Brooke stood in front of Brice's office door, pushed out a quick breath and raised her balled fist to knock, only she couldn't do it. She was suddenly hit with the memory of the first time she'd met Brice, in this very office.

She walked into the office to find the most handsome man she'd ever seen wearing an expensive-looking gray suit and wireless headphones staring at his computer. "Excuse me," Brooke said as she walked up to his desk, waving to try to get his attention.

Brice removed his headphones and quickly got to his feet. "May I help you?" His eyes roamed her body. Brooke fought the urge to look down to make sure her black pencil skirt, matching jacket and white blouse didn't have a stain or something on them. She was extremely happy she'd worn her five-inch heels to raise her five-foot-seven-inch frame, because she just knew he had to be over six feet tall.

Brooke looked up at the handsome man with a sparkle in his eyes and a smile, hoping her nervousness wasn't showing.

Dear Reader,

If you have read any of my work, you know how much I love showcasing unique family dynamics in a great sexy romance. The Kingsleys of Texas offers that and so much more.

In *Be My Forever Bride*, soon-to-be divorced couple Brice and Brooke Kingsley are forced to work together to ensure their company's financial standing with the IRS remains positive. In the process, secrets and lies are exposed, forcing this couple to reevaluate all their previous beliefs.

Please let me know how you liked Brice and Brooke's story. I love interacting with my readers. You can contact me on Facebook or Twitter, @kennersonbooks.

You've seen glimpses of Morgan Kingsley throughout the series. Coming soon is his full story.

Until then,

Martha

BE MY FOREVER
Bride

MARTHA
KENNERSON

H **HARLEQUIN**®KIMANI™ ROMANCE

Recycling programs
for this product may
not exist in your area.

ISBN-13: 978-1-335-21655-7

Be My Forever Bride

Copyright © 2018 by Martha Kennerson

For questions and comments about the quality of this book please contact us
at CustomerService@Harlequin.com.

Printed in U.S.A.

Martha Kennerson's love of reading and writing is a significant part of who she is, and she uses both to create the kinds of stories that touch your heart. Martha lives with her family in League City, Texas, and believes her current blessings are only matched by the struggle it took to achieve such happiness. To find out more about Martha and her journey, check out her website at www.marthakennerson.com.

As a writer, it is very important to me that my stories come from a place of real love and are based in some truths. I'd like to dedicate this story to my friend and muse, Danielle. Thank you for allowing me to share parts of your truth and journey. You have been a real inspiration.

Acknowledgments

I would be remiss if I didn't thank my online resources AboveMS.com and NationalMSSociety.org for all their valuable information.

Chapter 1

Brice Kingsley stood, flexing every muscle in his body to ensure he remained upright. Thanks to the news he'd just received, Brice was like a volcano ready to explode. The most conservative in his opinions and dress of the Kingsley brothers—CFO of his family's multi-billion-dollar oil and gas corporation—had traded in his usual business attire for a more casual look: blue jeans, a black button-down shirt and black leather loafers. He'd finally decided to take his brothers' advice to move on with his life and get past the fact that he'd be divorced soon. His first step was drinks with a few good friends and a couple of very beautiful women.

Brice flew out of his chair, which slid backward when he leaned forward and gripped the table with both hands as if he was holding back his desire to attack. The internal battle he was fighting between disbelief and rage had marred his features.

"What the hell did you say?" The words were out of Brice's mouth before he could stop them.

There were audible sighs from those sitting down and squeaking from chairs moving before the room fell silent. Brice looked down the long mahogany oval table, past the surprised faces of his eldest brother and two cousins. They sat wide-eyed in the large wingback chairs, staring at the target of his question.

The fair-skinned, wrinkle-free woman pushed her chair back and rose slowly. The shimmery gold gown she wore showcased an immaculate figure of a woman that didn't look anywhere near her fifty-four years. Victoria Kingsley, the matriarch of the family and CEO of Kingsley Oil and Gas, glared back at her third son.

Remembering whom he was speaking to, Brice straightened, returning to his full height of six feet, his hands fisting at his side. "What I meant to ask, was how could you make such a decision without discussing it with me first?" Brice knew better than to ask such a ridiculous question, but in his current state of shock and disbelief he really didn't know what else to say.

"Victoria, maybe I should—"

Victoria presented the palm of her right hand, stopping her sister, Elizabeth Kingsley, the more reasonable of the two when it came to handling their respective children by most accounts, from interfering and offering up what she knew would be a more sedated explanation for her decision.

Victoria exhaled noisily, collapsed her hands together and held them in front of her. "Let me see. The last time I checked, *I* was the CEO of Kingsley Oil and Gas and one of two—" she wiggled two fingers "—majority stakeholders. My decisions aren't up for discussion unless I say they are. This is a notification period. Brooke starts tomorrow!"

Brice knew how his mother ran her company, but he still couldn't understand how she could do something that she knew would be hard for him to handle. "I understand that, Mother, but this is my life we're talking about."

Victoria moved to the glass bar that sat in the corner of the room and poured herself a shot of Macallan whiskey. "No, what I made was a business decision. You're making it personal, son."

"So, your bringing Brooke back to work here isn't personal?" he asked, his tone hard. Twenty-seven-year-old Brooke Kingsley was a tax attorney, finance wizard and Brice's soon-to-be ex-wife.

Victoria took a sip of her drink. "Of course not. You know I don't do personal when it comes to business." Her eyes zeroed in on her sister. "Not anymore, anyway. Brooke is excellent at what she does and she knows our company. There are too many people coming after us. The IRS is just the latest. With Keylan going back on the road with the team and taking Mia, another one of our valued employees, with him —"

"Of course he'll want his wife…his new family by his side. How many times did Alexander ever take a trip without you?" Elizabeth interjected, looking over her shoulder at her sister.

"I can remember one time in particular and so should you." Victoria looked down at her bare ring finger and tossed back the rest of her drink.

Elizabeth turned away and muttered, "I do. Sorry, Victoria."

Victoria poured herself another whiskey and her sister a glass of wine. "The point is we need people we can trust, helping with this fight." She smiled down at her sister and handed her the wine.

"Are you sure you can trust her?" Brice knew his question was coming from a place of hurt and anger, but it was the only ammunition he had left.

Victoria returned to her seat. "May I?" Elizabeth asked.

"Please." Victoria raised her glass.

"Brice, darling, I understand that you might be a little apprehensive about having Brooke around again, but we need her help. Maybe you two can work out your issues," she replied, her smile faint.

Brice loved his aunt's sweet spirit and he appreciated her glass-half-full approach when it came to most things, but this time he had to stand firm. Working with Brooke would be more difficult than anyone seemed to understand. Brice puffed out his chest and went stone-faced.

"If she comes back, I won't work with her," he announced.

Victoria sat forward, placed her drink on the table and leered at her son. The room's temperature seemed to drop several degrees. "What does that mean exactly? Are you resigning from your role as CFO?"

"What?" Brice's forehead creased. He didn't know what he meant, but it certainly wasn't that.

"Of course not, Mother," COO Alexander quickly said, scowling at Brice, who stood in silence with his hands in his pockets. "Everyone just needs to calm down and take a breather."

Victoria's cell phone rang. She removed the phone from her Hermès bag and answered it with the brief statement, "I'll be down in a moment." Victoria rose from her seat and this time everyone followed suit, except her sister, who remained in her chair. Victoria returned her phone to her purse, leaned over and kissed her sister on the cheek.

"Have a nice evening, Victoria," Elizabeth said with a half-smile.

"I always do. I trust you can—"

"I'll take care of everything here," Elizabeth promised.

Victoria offered Alexander her cheek, which he kissed before saying, "Everything's going to be fine."

Victoria moved to Kristen Kingsley, Elizabeth's only

daughter and their company's vice president of general operations. "I expect those files on my desk first thing in the morning," she instructed before giving her a hug.

"Yes, ma'am," Kristen eagerly replied.

Victoria sent Travis, Kristen's twin brother and one of two Kingsley heirs that didn't work for the company, an air-kiss across the table. "See your mother home safely before you head back to that ranch of yours."

"Always," he promised.

When Victoria finally made her way to the door where Brice was now standing, she placed her right hand on his chest and stared up at him. Brice's eyes scanned her face for any signs of what was coming but she stood stone-faced.

"The next time you threaten me with not doing your job, you had better have a letter of resignation to offer otherwise, I will fire you, son. Understand?" Brice gave a quick nod. "Good." Victoria dropped her hand, offered her cheek, which he kissed, and left the room.

"Dammit, Brice, what the hell's wrong with you? You're twenty-eight, not a goddamn impulsive eighteen-year-old," Alexander scolded his brother, making his way over to the bar.

"Language," Elizabeth stated, taking a sip of her wine.

"Pour me one too, Alexander," Travis requested, taking his seat. "Aunt Victoria is an OG and she doesn't play. I think she really would've fired you," he concluded.

"I would have," Kristen offered, collecting her things.

"Of course you would have, sis. You're just like her."

Elizabeth gave the evil eye to her bickering children. "That's enough, you two."

Brice leaned forward against the chair he'd long ago abandoned and dropped his head. He knew his brother was right; he was being impulsive. Brice couldn't believe how quickly things had turned with his mother, all because of the emotions Brooke invoked that he still couldn't control. How was he going to handle working day-in and day-out with her?

"Mother, I'll take you home," Kristen offered. "Let these two see if they can talk some sense into Brice."

Elizabeth rose from her chair and smoothed out her green flower-print dress. "That's a great idea, darling, and maybe on our way home I can convince you to add a little more color to your wardrobe." She scrunched up her face at the black pantsuit Kristen wore.

"Black *is* a color, Mother."

"No, it's not. Black is a statement."

"It's in the coloring box," Kristen said sarcastically. "What about Travis? He's wearing black jeans and a black shirt. I don't hear you threatening him with a lesson on the coloring wheel."

"We're not talking about your brother," she declared, hugging and kissing her son and nephew before walking out of the conference room with her daughter on her heels.

Brice dropped down in his chair and accepted the glass his brother offered. "Thanks, A."

"You okay?" Alexander stood, swirling his drink in his glass.

"Not really," Brice admitted.

"Well, you need to do whatever you have to so you can *get* okay. You have got to pull it together. Another performance like that one and I'll fire you myself," he said, tossing back his drink.

Brice mirrored his brother's actions, allowing the gold liquid to slide down his throat, hoping it would burn some sense into him. "I will. I guess it was just the shock of knowing no matter what I did or said, I couldn't get my wife to even talk to me, yet my mother was able to convince her to come back to work for us. It's as if nothing ever happened between us, let alone a marriage."

"You know I understand how you feel, but you have to rise above it. You have a job to do," Alexander reminded Brice.

"You know what you need." Travis smiled like he had a secret he was dying to spill.

"What's that?" Brice knew he shouldn't ask, but at this point, he needed all the help he could get.

"You should find a bar and look for something soft and sweet to spend the night with. Lose yourself in someone for a while before you have to see Brooke again." Travis shrugged. "It couldn't hurt."

The mere idea of being with another woman sexually was making his stomach hurt. He had just given himself permission to have drinks with another woman. "Thanks, but I'll pass."

"Let's go, Travis. He needs a minute," Alexander observed.

Brice leaned back in his chair and closed his eyes. His mind flashed back to the last time he had seen Brooke: after he'd returned home from getting her favorite meal, only to find that she'd left him via a short note. It had taken Brice nearly two months to convince Eddie, the husband of Brooke's best friend, to help him in his efforts to find his wife. When he found out she was in Paris, he flew over to try and figure out what was really going on. He hadn't bought her explanation that they had gotten married too fast and that she wasn't ready to settle down. Brooke's actions during their six-month marriage told him the very opposite. They had even started having discussions about starting a family.

Brice remembered exactly how he'd felt the day he walked into the restaurant of the Hôtel Barrière Le Fouque along the Champs-élysées, one of Paris's most historic locations. The café was decorated with studio style portraits of popular actors and directors from several decades. The tables, accompanied by red velvet chairs, were dressed in fine white linen, expensive porcelain china and crystal. The room screamed romance and he knew Brooke would have loved it.

When Brice had spotted Brooke sitting at a table, holding up her head with her left hand, gazing into the eyes of another man he hadn't recognized who was caressing her wrist, his blood boiled as he stood out of her view watching and he knew his marriage was over. The pain of that memory jolted him forward. "No, she wasn't ready to settle down. It's time to move on."

Chapter 2

Brooke sat on the balcony of her suite at Houston's Hotel ZaZa, located in the heart of the museum district. She smiled in spite of the ache in her heart at the memories of all the times she and Brice had enjoyed their weekends getting lost in the cultural experiences there. Brooke still couldn't believe she had found a man who enjoyed what some found to be geeky activities—exploring museums and enjoying live performances in the park—as much as she did. She sipped her coffee and nibbled on different pastries as she watched the sunrise spread its rays over the city when she heard her door lock turn.

She heaved a sigh because she knew the silence of her morning was now over. "Good morning, Lori," she called out. Lori Murphy was Brooke's executive assistant and one of the few people she actually called a friend. Growing up in the foster care system made it difficult for Brooke to get close to people.

"Good morning. It's seven o'clock—why aren't you

dressed yet?" Lori questioned as she walked out onto the balcony in a gray suit and matching heels, her sandy blond hair in a tight bun.

"You look nice," Brooke complimented.

"Thanks. Shouldn't you get a move on?" Lori encouraged.

"I just needed a little more time with my friends *calm* and *quiet* before we have to take on the Kingsleys again. You know how daunting it can be, working for that family," she teased.

"I still don't understand why you accepted this assignment. May I?" she asked, admiring the many types of bread and fruits Brooke had to offer.

"Yes, of course." Brooke pushed the room service cart toward Lori. "I had no choice. We're still under contract with Kingsley Oil and Gas. A fact she reminded me of when she called me in Paris. Victoria's not the type of businesswoman to let someone walk away from a commitment because the situation may be a little uncomfortable."

"You're right about that, but she did set you up in a nice place. This balcony with a two-person tub and bed-like lounge seating is fantastic and awfully romantic. I'd kill to have those black-and-white chandeliers," she proclaimed, looking over her shoulder into the living room. Lori started eating her food as she walked back into the suite.

Brooke rose from her seat and followed after her. "Yes, she did. This place screams Victoria. It's pure over-the-top luxury."

"Don't forget about that beautiful black ceiling," she reminded Brooke, looking up.

"How could I?" She tightened her robe.

Lori popped a piece of fruit in her mouth. "Why'd she put you up in a hotel, anyway? And why here when there's a chain hotel right across from their building?"

"This is one of the Kingsleys' investment properties and providing accommodations is part of the contract."

"I know but I think you should go back to your house."

"That's Brice's house now. I left, remember?"

"I realize that," Lori said, shaking her head. "You could've stayed with me, you know."

"I know, but we see enough of each other working together. Speaking of work, is everything ready?"

"Everything but you," Lori answered, checking her watch.

"I'll go change." Brooke walked into the bedroom and looked down at the navy blue St. John long sleeve notched-collar suit jacket and its matching short sleeve dress and moaned. Over the last few months, Brooke had begun to dress more casually since she'd taken on a smaller less public role within the company. "This outfit is conservative and professional, just the way Victoria prefers it."

Brooke removed her robe and pulled her dress over a lace La Perla bra and underwear set. They gave her an added level of confidence and it was her sexy secret…a secret that used to be hers and Brice's. The thought sent a wave of sadness through her body that she had to immediately shake off before it took root. She slipped her feet into a pair of Christian Louboutin shoes and twirled in the mirror and said, "Welcome back… Some things never change."

She moved to the bathroom where she pulled her hair up into a tight bun and lightly made up her face. Brooke looked down at the three medicine bottles that sat next to her multi-vitamins and birth control pill and released an audible sigh. "Well, almost…"

"Knock-knock," Lori called out before she entered the room.

"I'm ready," Brooke replied, stepping out of the bathroom.

"Wow, you look great."

"Thanks. Good thing you insisted on the new wardrobe. My old business clothes would have never fit thanks to those fifteen pounds I never intended to lose," she confessed, walking back into the living room where she poured herself a glass of orange juice.

"Too bad Victoria won't adopt a more business casual approach at the office."

"Yeah, too bad." Brooke tossed back her handful of meds and washed them down with the orange juice.

"The car is here and Damon is already at the office," Lori advised. Damon Watts was a tax specialist and associate at Brooke's consulting firm. "That should go over well with Brice." Brooke grabbed her purse and briefcase. "Let's go."

The short ride from Brooke's hotel to the Kingsley offices was over in what seemed like a blink of an eye. Brooke exited the town car and stood in front of the office, looking up at the fifty-story glass building. "This place makes me feel so small," she said to herself. *In more ways than one.*

"I know. You can't even see the top floors for the clouds," Lori observed.

"Let's get this over with." Both women walked into the lobby with their heels clicking on the black-and-white marble floors, announcing their presence to the guards.

"This place isn't nearly as busy as I remembered," Lori stated, as they approached the guard station that sat in front of a giant water wall.

"Of course not—it's nearly nine. Everyone here starts work between seven and eight," Brooke explained.

"Good morning, Mrs. Kingsley," the guard greeted.

Brooke had the urge to turn to see if Victoria or Elizabeth was standing behind her but she knew better. She knew exactly whom the guard was addressing as he smiled down at her. If that wasn't enough of a giveaway, the tingling that ran down her spine to her private parts most certainly was. "Good morning."

"Here are your credentials and security pass," he explained, handing them to Brooke.

"Thank you."

The guard turned to Lori. "Miss Murphy, I assume?"

"Yes, I'm Lori Murphy."

"These are for you. Mr. Watt has arrived already."

"Thank you," Lori replied, clipping her badge to her jacket.

"Please follow me to the elevators." The guard swiped his pass in front of the keypad and the elevator door opened. "As a reminder, Mrs. Kingsley, please enter the elevator one at a time."

Brooke thanked him before they entered. Lori followed her in and when the doors closed, she asked, "What was that all about?"

"Additional security. The doors activate the body-scanning device. That's why there's a slight pause before we start moving," she explained, hitting the buttons to the forty-eighth and fiftieth floor.

"Wow, they take their security around here very seriously."

"Yes they do. The Kingsleys have a lot to protect," she mumbled.

"How do you feel?"

Brooke could see the concern written all over Lori's face. "I'm fine. We'll be in and out of here in a few weeks and then it's back to Paris."

"I still can't believe you're moving your base to Paris."

Brooke shrugged. "With the success of my business, I can work anywhere, so why not France?"

The elevator came to a stop on the forty-eighth floor. Brooke handed her things to Lori. "You not coming?" Lori asked with a deep frown.

"I can't put this off any longer. I'll see you in a bit."

Lori stepped out of the elevator and Brooke plastered on a fake smile, hoping to calm her friend's fears while she stood and watched the doors close. Brooke knew how worried Lori would be at the thought of her being alone with Brice. Lori understood how Brooke's unresolved feelings for him could induce a negative physical reaction. However, Brooke also knew that if she didn't address the very large elephant in the building first thing this morning, her time there would be even more difficult.

Brice stood in front of his vertical desk that sat on the left side of his traditional mahogany one in front of the wall of windows. He was trying to concentrate on the documents before him but failing measurably. He'd barely gotten four hours of sleep the night before, anticipating seeing Brooke again. It had been three months since she left him and a month since he'd seen her in Paris. Brice was experiencing a whirlwind of emotions, none of which he could seem to bring under control.

"Excuse me, boss," his beautiful and curvy research assistant interrupted, standing in his doorway.

Brice smiled at the tall and lovely sight before him. A fact that others had pointed out in hopes that he would consider dating her and move on from Brooke. Most people couldn't see past her beauty to her brilliant mind. "Come in, Amy."

"Everything's set up for Mrs. Kingsley and her team's arrival."

Amy's words were like a shot to the gut. He used to love it when people addressed his wife by his last name. Now, hearing it was like nails on a chalkboard. "Thank you."

"Can I get you anything?"

"Yes, actually." Brice handed her a list of cases he needed researched. "Those are all relevant to the new pipeline. We need to make sure we cover our bases with the affected communities. We don't want the EPA back in our lives."

Amy smiled. "Really? I thought you wanted to handle that project on your own."

Brice moved to his stationary desk, sat down and fired up his computer. "Yeah, well, I'm a little distracted," he admitted, which was an understatement. "Also, can you call my cousin Kristen and tell her I'll need to take a rain check on dinner tonight?"

"Sure thing, and I'll be down the hall in the law library if you need me."

"Thanks and close the door behind you, please." Brice only wished he could stay hidden in his office during Brooke's short stay.

Brooke stood in front of Brice's office door, pushed out a quick breath and raised her balled fist to knock—only she couldn't do it. She was suddenly hit with the memory of the first time she'd met Brice in that very office nearly three years earlier.

She walked into the office to find the most handsome man she'd ever seen wearing an expensive-looking gray suit and wireless headphones while he stared at his computer. Brooke had never found herself at a loss for words, yet the man before her, with his light-colored skin, dark, curly hair and full, sexy lips, were wreaking havoc on her system. "Excuse me," Brooke said, walking up to his desk and waving, trying to get his attention.

Brice removed his headphones and quickly got to his feet. "May I help you?" His eyes roamed her body. Brooke fought the urge to look down to make sure her black pencil skirt, matching jacket and white blouse didn't have a stain or something on it. She was extremely happy she'd worn her five-inch heels to raise her five-foot seven-inch frame because she just knew he had to be at least six-feet tall.

Brooke looked up at the handsome man with a sparkle in his eyes and a smile on his lips, hoping her nervousness wasn't showing. After all, this was her first major client for her new firm. "I apologize if I'm intruding. They sent me up from downstairs but no one's out front. My name is Brooke Smith and I'm looking for Mr. Brice Kingsley."

"I'm Brice Kingsley," he replied, smiling and showing off a beautiful set of white teeth.

Brooke extended her hand. "Pleased to meet you."

Brice gave it a small shake. "Likewise, but it's six fifteen in the morning. Why are you here so early?"

"I like to get started early while it's still quiet. It's usually the only time I can enjoy my jazz at full blast before others get in and I have to wear my headphones," she explained.

The corners of his mouth quirked up. "You like jazz?"

Surprise was written all over his face. "I love it," she assured him.

"I do too. Please have a seat. Can I get you some coffee?"

"Yes, cream and sugar, please," Brooke replied, taking a seat in one of the large round chairs in front of his desk.

Brice walked over to a small table next to his desk where a vintage coffee station had been set up. He poured her a cup, pulled a vanilla-flavored creamer from the desk drawer along with several packets of sugar. He handed her the cup and placed the cream, sugar and a stirrer straw in front of her.

"Please." He directed her attention to the condiments. "Help yourself."

"Thank you." Brooke added the sugar and creamer to her coffee and took a sip. "Very good."

"You sound surprised." His brows were standing at attention.

"Honestly, I am." Brooke smiled over her cup at the amused look on his face. "But I'm also impressed. A lot of men can't make a good cup of coffee."

"You have to have the right mixture of water to bean," Brice explained.

"Now I'm really impressed," she admitted. "Most men don't know that."

Brice took a seat behind his desk. "I'm the one impressed. Your catch saved us millions of dollars. I still can't believe our former tax accountants had been using several incorrect forms and overlooking valuable deductions. I can't imagine your bosses at the IRS are very happy with you."

"Not at all. They fired me."

"I'm sorry to hear that," he said, frowning.

"Don't be. If they hadn't fired me, Victoria wouldn't have convinced me to come work for her."

"But only as a consultant. I understand you wouldn't come on board full-time." He gave her a quizzical look.

"No offense, but I want to be my own boss. I don't want to be tied down to one company. Thankfully, your mother understood that and hired me anyway. Kingsley is my first client."

Brice raised his coffee cup. "Here's to a long and fruitful relationship."

Brooke smiled and raised her cup. "Shall we get started?"

Brooke broke away from the past, pushed her shoulders back, raised her hand and knocked on the door. "Come in."

Chapter 3

Brooke opened the door and walked into the office to find Brice seated behind his desk, signing several documents. "Did you forget something, Amy?"

The sound of his voice sent waves of desire throughout her body, just like they had from the first moment they met. She'd missed it… She'd missed him. "It's not Amy, Brice," Brooke replied, closing the door behind her, knowing this conversation wasn't for the public.

Brice dropped his pen, raised his head and sat back in his seat. "Brooke," he said, his face expressionless.

"Do you have a moment for a quick chat?" She tried to project confidence when in reality she was a nervous wreck inside. Her heart was beating so fast she just knew the whole building could hear it.

Brice tilted his head slightly to the right and his forehead crinkled. "You tell me after six months of what I thought was a wonderful marriage that you want out. I convince you to give us time to work things out, at least

I thought I had, and go out for your favorite seafood only to come back to find that you've left me with a note." He leaned forward slightly. "You disappear for three months, only communicating through your lawyer, and now you want to chat." His tone was hard but even.

"I... I—"

"Sure, please, have a seat." His words were laced with disdain and sarcasm.

Brooke moved forward on unsteady legs, reaching for the support of a chair. She swallowed hard. "You make it sound so—"

"So what? Honest? Is that not what happened?"

"I didn't want to fight. Not then and certainly not now," she explained, trying to hold his angry glare.

"What *do* you want, Brooke?" Brice asked, sitting back in his chair.

"It's simple. I'd like to get through these next several weeks as painlessly as possible. We're both professionals with a job to do."

Brice sat up in his chair. "That we are." He reached into his desk drawer and pulled out a manila envelope. "We can start by you signing the settlement papers so the lawyers can move forward with the divorce."

He slid the envelope to Brooke. "I told you I don't want your money. I just want to keep my name."

"You mean *my* name, and I'm sure you do. It's not like Brooke Smith would bring in the big clients."

Brooke could nearly see the anger radiating from his body and he had every right to be furious with her, especially with the cowardly way she'd handled things but she felt she had no choice. Brooke thought her past, specifically the things she had done to put herself through school, and her present health issues would be too much to ask anyone to handle. Brooke knew how bad her request sounded, but she couldn't tell him the real reason she wanted to remain a Kingsley—it was the only way she'd always have a connection to him and his family. They were the two things she never had before and didn't think she ever would again.

"The only way you get to keep my name is if you take the settlement."

"I don't want or need your money. I can take care of myself," she reiterated.

"I don't give a damn if you want the money or not. It's a few million dollars—give it to a charity if you like. I won't ever be accused of not taking care of you," he stated matter-of-factly.

"Fine!" Brooke opened the envelope and pulled out the documents. "Got a pen I can borrow?"

"Sure." Brice handed her the Montblanc she'd given him last year for his birthday. He handed her the pen and their eyes met, and for a brief moment, Brooke thought they'd softened until he broke contact and reached for his buzzing phone. Brooke signed in all the highlighted spots. She returned the documents to the envelope, handed it and his pen back to him. "Happy?"

"Hardly. Just one more thing. We'd appreciate it if any extracurricular activity you may have going on is kept under wraps."

"Excuse me?" Her eyebrows stood at attention.

"Just continue to be discreet and so will I."

Brooke's heart sank when she caught on to what he was talking about. Although, Brooke wasn't entirely sure what he meant about *her* activities, she wanted to kick herself for being hurt by the idea of Brice moving on with his life. It's what she wanted…what she thought was best. Brooke couldn't get passed the lump in her throat to speak so she simply nodded.

"I'll get the papers to the lawyers right away. In sixty days, you'll be several million dollars richer and free of me. All just in time for our first anniversary."

"Can you not do that?" Brooke looked down at her intertwined hands lying in her lap, hoping to hide the slight tremor.

"Do what?"

Brooke raised her head and met his leer. "Act like a petulant child."

Brice raised his chin and narrowed his eyes but quickly relaxed his face. "Absolutely. We will keep things professional and limit our interactions."

"Fine. Maybe we can get through this almost painlessly," Brooke said, rising slowly from her chair. The last thing she wanted was for her legs to give out from under her. Brice stood, walked around his desk and came to stand in front of her. "We both know in our business…the world of finance…a world of precision, 'almost' doesn't count."

Brooke looked up into Brice's eyes and they were no longer devoid of emotion; they had softened. She actually had a sliver of hope that maybe they could salvage some type of friendship from the mess she'd made. They had been close before anything else and she missed him.

"Excuse me, Brice," a familiar voice interrupted. Brooke turned toward the door and saw Amy standing there, smiling at Brice with an excited look on her face as if she couldn't wait to see him or something.

Before Brooke knew it, her old insecurities about Amy resurfaced. Their old arguments that Brice had dismissed as ridiculous and a growing friendship that the two shared annoyed Brooke to no end. Without warning all types of nonsense came flying out of her mouth. "Amy, you're still here? Shouldn't your internship be up by now? Don't tell me you didn't pass your class." *So much for not acting like a child.* Brooke could feel Brice's eyes on her, but she kept her own on Amy.

"No, I passed and graduated *magna cum laude*, in fact." Amy frowned at Brice.

"Amy works for me now," Brice explained with a confused look on his face.

"Does she now?" Brooke murmured.

"Do you need anything, Amy?" Brice asked.

"It can wait. I just needed to talk to you about the dinner—"

"We're still on, right?" His eyes jumped between her and Brooke.

"Yes…of course," she replied, her smile widening.

Brooke felt sick and needed to escape. "Don't let me interrupt. I have to get to work, anyway." She turned and walked out the door.

"What was that all about?" Amy asked, bug-eyed.

"Sorry about that. It's just…" Brice ran his hand through his hair. He felt awful for using Amy in such a way and misleading Brooke. But the hurt and anger he tried to suppress surfaced at the thought of Brooke moving on with someone else, especially while he'd been pining after her, and made him want to strike back.

"I get it. You wanted a little payback for something she did. It's not my business, but if you want to talk, I'm here," she offered.

"Thanks, but I'm good. About what I said…" Brice rubbed the back of his neck.

Amy held up both hands. "No worries. You're fine and all, but you're not my type."

Brice laughed and went to sit behind his desk. "I'm not?"

"Nope, but your cousin Travis on the other hand…" she informed him, smiling.

"Yeah, well, I hate to burst your bubble but you're a bit young for him."

"I'm only four years younger than you," she reminded him.

"Yes, and six years younger than Travis. Trust me, you're too young."

Amy sat in one of the chairs that faced his desk. "I know. He already told me."

Brice frowned. "He did? When?"

"When I asked him out," she stated nonchalantly.

Brice chuckled and shook his head. "Fearless…"

"No disrespect, boss, but why was your ex being such a B toward me, anyway?"

"She's always thought you had a crush on me," he explained.

"Hardly…"

Brice checked his buzzing phone. "What did you want to tell me about Kristen's dinner?"

"She needed to cancel. Something came up."

"Oh, okay, thanks."

"How about I take you to dinner? That way, what you told your wife won't be a lie. Besides, you really do need to loosen up a bit. I know this great place downtown, so I'm not taking no for an answer," she insisted.

"I thought I was the boss."

Amy stood. "In this building you are, but at six, I'm in charge." She left the office laughing.

Brice was thankful for the distraction Amy brought. He enjoyed her youthful energy and the enthusiasm she had for their work. Brice could never understand why Brooke had felt threatened by Amy, who was more like a sister to him than anything. He knew making Brooke think he was seeing Amy socially was petty, but given the way Brooke had reacted toward Amy, Brice saw an opening to seek a little revenge for everything she'd put him through, especially since he chose not to confront her and the man she was with in Paris. Walking away was one of the hardest things he'd ever done. Only now, he felt horrible. Brice didn't want to see Brooke hurt, because no matter how hard he tried not to, he still cared about his wife.

Brooke entered the office that had been hers for over a year and found that it hadn't changed. The mahogany desk, which was a twin to the one in Brice's office, was still in the same spot where she'd left it on the left side of the room in front of her wall of bookshelves. Brooke hadn't wanted her desk placed in front of her windows, blocking her view of downtown Houston. Instead, she'd placed a small sofa and two chairs in the middle of the office—creating a small living room—so the views could be enjoyed by everyone visiting her. A ten-seater conference table had been placed across from the desk and living area and was adorned with six laptops, two printers and several boxes of documents that needed to be reviewed and audited.

"They didn't change a thing," Brooke announced, walking into the room.

"Nope, they didn't," Lori agreed, giving her friend the once-over. "Are you okay?"

"Yes... No, but I will be." Brooke took a seat at the table.

"We've organized things by quarter," Damon explained from his seat at the opposite end of the table.

"Thanks."

"Do you want to talk about whatever just happened between you and Brice?" Lori's jaw clenched and she crossed her arms at her chest.

"Not really," she said, breaking eye contact with her friend.

"If you change your mind—"

"He's actually dating Amy. Can you believe that?"

"Seriously?"

"Yep, but hey—" she shrugged "—if he wants to date a teenager, who am I to care? We're nearly divorced."

"What?" Lori's mouth flew open but quickly closed.

"Oh, yeah, I signed the papers, including the settlement."

"Good for you. Now you'll have plenty of money for whatever you might need and you get to keep the name too, I assume. What a good business move."

"I do and Brice agrees, but, you know that's not why I'm keeping his name," Brooke said defensively.

"I know." Lori's mouth twisted sideways.

Brooke could see the concern on her friend's face "Seriously, it's fine… I'm fine."

"If you say so. By the way, Peter is picking you up after work."

"What?"

Dr. Peter Schultz, a renowned neurologist from a family of physicians, was Brooke's doctor and foster brother. "You can't keep putting the man off, especially after he flew all the way to Paris to see you," Lori explained, taking a seat at the table across from Brooke.

"I can't deal with Peter right now. I need to focus on getting through this project." Brooke reached for several files.

"Peter wanted to meet you for lunch. He was prepared to send a car for you. I told him you already had lunch plans, which you do. I know how you like to work through lunch on the first day of a new project. I ordered Chinese for us and pizza for Damon."

"Good. Meat lovers, I hope?" Damon asked Lori.

"What else would I order for a carnivore like you?"

"Lori—"

"Peter needs to examine you."

Brooke presented her hands. "See, Mother, no tremors. I'm not tired and no muscle spasms."

"Good, now be sure to tell all that to Peter when he picks you up tonight. It's bad enough that only a handful of us know that you have multiple sclerosis and all you have to endure."

"You even said the only reason you told your foster brother is because he happens to be a neurologist and you needed a doctor you 'kind of' trusted," Damon added, using air quotes to emphasize his point. "Didn't you swear him to secrecy too? Making sure he didn't tell the rest of his family."

"Yes, she did." Lori nodded slowly. "I don't get it either. You were diagnosed nearly four months ago with a positive prognosis."

Yeah but for how long? With my luck, everything could change in a blink of an eye. "Guys, we've talked about this already. Growing up in the foster care system, you learn four major lessons." Brooke used the fingers of her right hand to count them off. "One, keep your material possessions close at all times. Two, keep all bed and bathroom doors locked when you're in the room. Three, expect the worst and consider yourself lucky if nothing bad happens. Four, the only person you can depend on is you. It took years for me to feel safe enough to open up even a little bit to people. Working day to day with you two made that easy."

"And we love and appreciate you for it too. We're here for you and always will be." Lori looked over at Damon, who offered his agreement in the form of a wide smile. "But you need to expand your circle of trust, my friend… at least by one."

Brooke knew exactly who she was referring to. She dropped her hands and released an audible sigh. "Remind me again why I keep you around."

"I'd like to know that myself," Damon interjected, clearly trying to bring more levity to the room.

Lori turned and stuck her tongue out at him. "Because I'm a brilliant assistant and a better friend."

"At least she didn't claim it was her legal expertise." Damon returned his eyes to the papers he was holding.

"That too," she countered, blinking her eyes dramatically.

"That's enough, children. Let's get to work," Brooke ordered.

The trio spent the next several hours going through the first month of all the Kingsley financial transactions and IRS filings. The hours seemed to fly by and before Brooke knew it, the sun had set. She raised her arms out and stretched. "Wow, it's after seven," she announced.

"Oh, no, I have to go." Lori started packing up her things. "John's going to kill me. We're supposed to meet with the wedding planner at seven-thirty."

"You better go, you too, Damon. Call it a night."

"You sure? I can stay until Dr. Schultz gets here," Damon offered.

Brooke gave a nonchalant wave. "Don't be silly. I'll be fine. I'm going to finish going through these bank statements and I'll call Peter."

"Are you sure?" Lori asked, standing by the door.

"I'm sure. Good work today, you two. I'll see you both tomorrow." Brooke stood and watched as they both walked out the door. She kicked off her shoes and flexed her feet. Brooke pulled her phone out of her purse and placed the call she'd been avoiding since she'd landed back in Texas.

"Good evening, Brooke. Is everything all right?" the sweet baritone voice asked.

"Yes, Doctor, everything is fine. I understand you're my ride back to the hotel tonight," Brooke replied sarcastically as she stood in front of the window, enjoying the sparkling lights of the city.

"I am. Are you ready?" Peter asked, laughing; Broke knew he was responding to the annoyance in her voice.

"Not yet. I have about another hour's worth of work left. Can you be here at eight-thirty?"

"Absolutely."

"Call me when you arrive," she advised before hanging up.

Brooke returned to her seat, where she picked up a bank statement and the highlighter and got back to her audit. She got through the last set faster than she'd expected. Brooke stood and started stacking all the files and papers when she heard the door open. She swirled around so fast she made herself dizzy. "Whoa…" She gripped the table to stay up right.

Brice was standing in the doorway and smirking. "You okay?"

"Yes. What are you doing here?" Brooke checked her watch. "It's nearly eight—is it past Amy's curfew?" *Dammit…*

Chapter 4

The corners of Brice's mouth turned up. He always loved her quick wit and the way Brooke's cheeks turned pink whenever she said something she wished she hadn't. Brooke had removed her jacket, her arms exposed, and she stood in her bare feet. Brice's eyes took their fill. Her naturally slim build was unusually thin, but he still thought she was the most beautiful woman he'd ever seen.

"Funny. No, her choice of restaurant was not really my taste."

Brooke shrugged. "That's what you get for dating a toddler."

Brice leaned into the door frame. "Amy's no toddler."

Brooke turned her back to him, saying, "I bet."

"Excuse me."

Brooke slid her feet back into her shoes, walked around the table and started gathering up her things. "It's none of my business, and who am I to question who you choose to spend your personal time with?"

"No, it's not. You lost that right the night you left."

Brooke raised her head and met his stormy gaze. "You're right, my apologies."

Brice pushed off the door frame and walked into the office. "No problem—"

"I just don't see what you two could possibly have in common."

"You'd be surprised." Brice didn't want to continue this line of questioning. His exaggeration was making him uncomfortable. It was time to change the subject. "So how was your first day back? I trust you have everything you need."

"I do." Their eyes collided at the familiar phrase they'd recited not so long ago. "I mean, everyone's been very helpful."

"So we should meet our established three-month time-frame?" he questioned, trying to keep his business persona intact when his traitorous body was responding to Brooke on a more personal level.

"Barring any surprises, yes, we should," she reassured him confidently.

"Good. Have you eaten yet? There's no reason we can't be civil."

"Actually—" Brooke's cell phone rang. "Excuse me."

Brice saw a face he'd hoped he would never have to see again pop up on Brooke's phone.

"You here?" Brooke answered.

"Yes," Peter replied. "I didn't want to give you a chance to leave without me."

Brooke laughed. "I wouldn't do that. I'll be right down." She ended the call and returned the phone to her purse.

"Sounds like you have other plans." Brice pressed his lips together, preventing himself from asking questions he didn't really want the answers to.

Brooke nodded. "But thanks for the offer... Rain check?"

"Sure." Brice placed both hands in his pocket as he tried to keep a straight face, attempting to hide the disappointment that he wanted to kick himself for even feeling. "I'll walk you out."

"That's really not necessary, but thank you." Brooke reached for her jacket, only Brice beat her to it. He held it out and Brooke slipped both arms through each sleeve. Brice's hands briefly rested on the small of her back as his senses were attacked by the scent of jasmine wafting from Brooke's hair. Brooke looked over her shoulder, gazed up at him and whispered, "Thank you, Brice," before stepping away.

Brice knew she was thanking him for more than helping with her coat. They'd rarely had disagreements, but when they did it usually ended quickly. Her kind heart just wouldn't let things fester, which was another reason why he'd found her actions so unbelievable. Citing that their marriage was an impulse, she'd requested it be annulled, a request he flatly refused. Brooke's desire to keep his name was the only leverage he had to slow things down so he could try and find out what was really going on between them.

"You're welcome."

They walked out of the office and made their way to the elevator where they descended in silence. They exited the elevator and walked through the nearly empty lobby. Brice eyed the tall olive-skinned man leaning against a black town car with his arms crossed.

"Your ride?" Brice asked, setting his mouth in a tight line.

"Yes."

Brice stopped short of the exit. "Have a good evening."

"You too," Brooke replied as she walked out the door.

The last thing Brice wanted was to stand there and watch as his rival greeted Brooke with an extended hand and helped her into his car. But Brice's feet were glued to that spot. He knew he should walk away but for the life of him, he couldn't figure out how to get his feet to work.

After assisting Brooke into her seat, Peter walked around to the other side of the car and slid behind the wheel. "Are you okay?" he asked with a concerned look on his face.

"Yes, and I really wish everyone would stop asking me that question," Brooke snapped back, staring out the car window.

Peter pulled out into the traffic and drove the short distance to Brooke's hotel in silence. He parked in front and cut the engine. Peter shifted his body toward Brooke. "You ready to talk about it?"

"Talk about what?" Brooke frowned.

"Whatever it is that's got you so upset."

"I thought you were my neurologist, not my therapist," she replied, collapsing her hands together in her lap.

"Right now, I'm prepared to be both."

Brooke cleared her throat. "It was just a lot harder than I expected. Seeing Brice again, I mean."

"Have you given any more thought to telling him the truth?"

"All the time, but the end result is always the same. Can we go upstairs and get this over with, Doctor?"

Brooke walked through the lobby of the hotel with Peter at her side. When she heard her name being called, Brooke turned toward the sound.

"Excuse me, Mrs. Kingsley," the concierge called as he approached, holding a large manila envelope.

"Yes?" she replied.

"This was delivered this afternoon. I was instructed to hand it to you personally."

Brooke's heart sank as she guessed it held her copy of the divorce agreement. "Thank you," she whispered, accepting the package. "Let me…" Brooke fumbled with her purse as tears burnt the back of her eyes. Her whole body went numb and it had nothing to do with her multiple sclerosis.

Brooke's mind jumped back in time to the day she'd attended her sister-in-law China's baby shower. It was the day that changed the course of her life. China looked especially beautiful; she was glowing like the moon on a clear night and if Brooke could have disappeared, she would have. She had just received her MS diagnosis and had been informed that pregnancy for her might not be possible, depending on her therapy. Her doctors explained that she could have a small window should she want to try and have a baby of her own, but they needed to determine her therapy as soon as possible. Brooke's difficult childhood and pessimistic attitude toward having her own happily ever after only allowed her to believe the worst.

After receiving such devastating news, Brooke had been in no mood to celebrate but she had to show her support for China and Alexander. After all, they were her family now. Brooke smiled through the games and forced down delicious food and champagne. She held back tears when everyone asked when she and Brice were going to start having babies. It was only after people started taking bets on when that might happen that she found a reason to excuse herself.

It was that day—along with a not-so-veiled threat to expose her past to her new family—that Brooke had decided to leave Brice. She thought he deserved someone better than her. In her mind, her diagnosis just confirmed what she'd always known: She'd never be truly happy. Brooke hadn't had a happy childhood, so how could she have a happy adult life?

"I got it." Peter opened his leather bag, pulled out his wallet and handed the concierge a generous tip. Brooke stood, staring down at the envelope. "Let's get you upstairs."

Peter took Brooke by the elbow and led her to the elevator. She held the envelope to her chest as tears welled in her eyes. They rode up in silence, exited the elevator and walked the short distance to her door. Brooke crossed the threshold, wandered into the living room and gingerly sat on the sofa.

Peter went into the kitchen, removed a bottle of water from the refrigerator, twisted off the cap and came back into the main room, handing the bottle to Brooke. "Drink."

Brooke took several sips. "Thanks." She set the envelope on the coffee table.

"Do you need a minute?"

Brooke took a deep breath and released it slowly. "No, let's get this exam done."

Peter removed a penlight and reflex hammer from his bag and placed them on the table. He stood and moved to the middle of the room. "You know the drill."

Brooke kicked off her shoes, then went and stood in front of Peter. She presented her hands palms down. "No tremors."

"Good."

She extended her arms out to her side and brought her right index fingers to her nose. "I feel like I'm taking a sobriety test."

"You say that every time," he reminded Brooke. "Left hand, please."

Brooke complied. "What's next?"

"You know, walk the line. Heel to toe, please."

Brooke released a loud moan. "Here goes nothing."

Brooke completed the task, but it took her longer than normal because she was tired and her muscles were reminding her of that fact.

"Not bad. Take a seat," he instructed.

Brooke returned to the sofa and took several sips from her water bottle. She felt like she'd just run a mile full out. Peter checked her reflexes and responses to light. "Everything looks good," he announced as he made notes on his tablet.

"I told you when you came to Paris that I was fine and symptom-free." Peter gave her the side-eye. "Well, mostly symptom-free."

"We talked about this. You're fortunate that you don't have the more common symptoms of motor problems, cognitive issues, severe pain and sexual dysfunction, to name a few, but that can change over time. While your symptoms aren't chronic, flare-ups can be triggered by stress. The fatigue, muscle pain, numbness and tingling in your limbs can be hard on your system."

"I know all of this, Peter." Brooke reached for her room-service menu.

Peter continued as though she hadn't said a word. "And while your symptoms will disappear and remain repressed when you remove the triggers, let's try to avoid them altogether, shall we? Otherwise, you'll keep repeating the cycle."

Brooke gave Peter a two-fingered salute. "Yes, sir."

Peter packed his bag. "One more thing. I know you think you're doing what's best for your husband, but if I were him, I'd want to know the truth. MS isn't a death sentence."

"I know that, Doctor, but it can be a long and difficult journey." *Not to mention having to deal with my colorful past. That's too much to ask of anyone, no matter how much they love you.*

"Yes, it can, but it can also be filled with lots of love and even children."

"I don't want to talk about this. I'm ordering food. Care for anything?" Brooke picked up the menu and started browsing through it.

"No, thank you, and I think we should," he said, taking the menu from Brooke. "Having MS shouldn't stop you from getting pregnant or having a healthy pregnancy. Now, if you were in the middle of a specialized treatment plan, that would be a different story and even then, we'd just suspend the treatments until you delivered. You're nowhere near that, either."

Not with my luck. A successful career is about as close as I'm going to get to having a family. "I understand you're trying to help, but I've made my decision. I'm not dragging Brice into this mess of a life I have. He's better off finding someone without so much baggage," she declared, reaching for the menu.

"Fine, but don't you think that's a decision your husband has a right to make?"

"No! Now if you're done—"

"Actually—"

"With your role as my medical doctor, I'd like to call it a night. I need to eat and get my rest. Doctor's orders," she reminded him, rising from her spot on the sofa.

Peter exhaled loudly. "Fine. I may be your doctor, Brooke, but you're also my family. I just want you to be happy and it's obvious you're not happy about losing the only man you've ever loved."

"I know you do, and I'll always be grateful to you and your family for taking me in that last year I was in high school. Yours was the only foster home I ever felt safe in."

"Just think about what I said."

"Okay. You know, you really need to find a life of your own and stop worrying about mine."

"So my mother keeps telling me." He picked up his bag and walked to the door. "See you in a couple of months, unless you need me before then."

"I won't. Thanks, Peter."

Brooke closed the door and suddenly she wasn't hungry, but she knew she had to put some food in her stomach before she took her medicine. She went to the phone and ordered something light. After placing the request, she went to the bedroom, undressed and took a quick shower. Brooke was standing in the middle of the bathroom, her body wrapped in a large towel, squeezing the excess water from her hair with another, when she heard her cell phone ring. She walked back into the bedroom, picked up her phone on the dresser and looked at the screen. The name read *unknown*. "Hello."

"I found you," a muffled voice replied.

"Who is this?" Brooke asked before the line went dead. "Kids." Brooke wrapped her hair in the towel, dried herself off and changed into a long nightshirt and shorts. She walked back into the living room and there was a knock on the door. "Who is it?"

"Room service," a soft voice replied.

Brooke opened the door and stood back as the waitress rolled in a small table. She lifted the lid from the plate and said, "Chicken salad sandwich on a croissant. Will that be all?"

"Yes, thank you."

She handed Brooke the bill to sign and took her exit. Brooke picked up the plate, sat on the sofa and stared down at the envelope that would change everything. She forced herself to eat half her sandwich until she started to feel anxious, so she placed the plate back on the table and wheeled it outside the door.

Brooke walked out onto the balcony and took a couple of deep breaths. She wrapped her arms around herself in an effort to contain her tremors. Her heart was racing and no matter how hard she fought, the dam broke and her tears fell. Brooke cried for the end of her marriage, for the fact that—as far as she was concerned and regardless of what the facts might have been—she'd never have children, but most of all, she cried because she knew she'd never stop loving Brice and somehow had to find a way to live with that realization.

Chapter 5

Brice circled and jabbed at the punching bag he had placed in the man cave he established in the lower level of the three-story house in the Houston Museum District he'd bought Brooke as a wedding present. It was a lovely starter home in the perfect location. He just recently turned the open concept lower level into the perfect getaway spot for a much-needed escape. Every time he walked upstairs, it was like the ghost of Christmas past, assaulting him with memories of the brief time he'd had there with Brooke.

He punched and kicked the freestanding bag until his arms, shoulders and legs screamed for surrender. Brice wiped the sweat from his brow with a towel as he walked to the small kitchenette and pulled out a large bottle from the refrigerator. He twisted off the cap and was gulping down water when he heard a knock on his door. *What now?*

"Who is it?" he called out harshly, not in the mood for visitors.

"It's me, Brice."

"Alexander?"

"Yeah, open up."

Brice moved past the large sectional sofa sitting in front of two medium-size ottomans that doubled as coffee tables and a fifty-inch screen television mounted to the wall as he made his way to the door. "What's up, A?" he asked, stepping aside, allowing his brother to enter.

"What's up with you?" Alexander asked.

When Alexander walked through the door, still wearing the same suit he'd had on at the office, Brice knew this wasn't a social call; something was definitely wrong. And if that wasn't enough, the twitching muscles in his brother's jaw certainly did.

"I'm good," Brice lied. "Want a beer?"

"No, thanks. Look, Brice, I can only imagine how hard this must be…working with Brooke, I mean."

"I know what you mean, man, and it's fine." He moved to his sofa and took a seat.

"You sure? Because we have a lot riding on making sure we're cool with the IRS and Brooke is the one person that can ensure that happens. Her IRS experience and history with our company aside, she's family."

"I'm sure. Damn, you sound more and more like Mother every day."

"Well, in this instance, she's right," he stated.

"I guess. KJ will be on in a few—want to stay and watch the game?"

"Not this time. I'll catch it at home, but first I have to pick up dinner and ice cream for China."

Brice smirked. "Lucky you."

"That I am," Alexander acknowledged, taking a seat next to his brother. "So, today was good?"

Brice saw the doubtful look on his brother's face. "Yes, it was. Brooke even signed the divorce agreement. I offered to take her to dinner but she had other plans…with another man."

"Ouch…"

"But in fairness I did make it seem like I was seeing Amy, so I guess we're even…kind of, anyway."

Alexander's eyebrows came to attention. "Amy, your research assistant?" Brice nodded. "And why would you do that?"

"Because I'm an idiot." Brice stood, walked to his refrigerator and pulled out a beer. He popped off the cap and took one long pull. Brice stood with his back to his brother. "I didn't know just how much I missed her until I saw her again, but I can't seem to get past my anger."

Alexander rose and turned toward Brice. "Look at me, man." Brice's shoulders dropped and he turned and met his brother's inquisitive gaze. "Look, if you want another shot with Brooke, you should just go for it. Remember the advice you gave me about China?"

"Yeah, but that was different." He took another pull from his bottle.

"How so?"

"You two have always had something special. It just took several years before you figured out what it was," Brice explained.

"You don't think what you and Brooke had was special?"

"I thought so…"

"Look, I can't tell you what to do, but I wouldn't be so quick to walk away if there's even the slightest chance she's your One."

"It's not just up to me, A. Besides, she's already moved on."

"You sure about that?"

"She left me, remember?" Brice finished off his beer,

tossed the bottle in the recycling bin and flopped back down on the couch.

"I remember. I also remember the BS 'you two got married too soon…too young' excuse she gave you too. I can't believe you're not digging deeper into that." His eyebrows snapped together.

Brice reached for the TV remote and placed his feet up on the ottoman. "She signed the papers. It's done."

"You're right. You are an idiot." Alexander moved toward the door. "Just be sure to keep it professional at the office."

"I'm over the shock. You know me, A. I'm a Kingsley and we're all about our business." Brice turned on the game.

"And that's what I'm afraid of, little brother. Later." Alexander walked out the door.

Brice hit the mute button. He laid his head back and closed his eyes, allowing his mind to drift back to a time when he'd tried to watch his brother KJ's game but Brooke had had something else planned…

Brice was in the living room sitting on the blue suede extra-long sofa that Brooke had insisted they needed, with his legs stretched out before him. In a gray T-shirt and a pair of long shorts, he was ready to coach his brother's team to victory from his new sofa. He sat back, watching the TV, when Brooke shouted down from upstairs, "Honey, you ready?"

"For what?" he replied. Hearing no response, he said, "Sure, call in whatever you want to eat, as long as they deliver."

Brooke laughed. The sound made him happy. Her laugh was one of the many things he loved about his new wife. "Cute," she said as she descended the steps, stopping halfway down. "What are you doing?"

Hearing the surprise in her voice but oblivious to her appearance, Brice called out, "Watching the NBA's pre-show. KJ's game starts in thirty minutes."

Brooke reached the bottom of the stairs and stood staring at him in silence. Brice's eyes shifted from the TV to his wife, who was standing there wearing a short black cocktail dress, strappy heels that showed off her sexy legs, and her hair and face made up like she was ready for a night of partying.

Brice's mind raced. He was trying to figure out what he'd missed. It's not date night. *Brice's body responded to the gorgeous sight before him and he quickly got to his feet. "Where are you going?"*

"I thought we were going dancing."

"Tonight? KJ's playing."

Brooke placed her hands on her hips. "You made these plans, remember?"

Brice quickly searched his mind and recollection of their brief conversation reared its ugly and badly timed head. "Oh, baby, you're right. I'm so sorry. I completely forgot." He picked up the remote and turned off the TV. "Give me fifteen minutes to change."

"Never mind." She walked farther into the living room.

"Sweetheart, you're all dressed up and ready to go. You look beautiful too." He started to move toward her.

"Thank you, but please sit back down."

Brice complied, expecting an argument would soon follow, only to receive the most pleasant surprise. "It's no big deal," she started to explain as she kicked off her shoes. She gifted Brice with a sexy smile. "I really wasn't in the mood to go out. However, I'd like something else from you."

Brice smiled up at his wife, waiting for the request that his body already knew; the front of his pants had tented.

Brooke's eyes dropped to his crotch and she bit her lip. "Exactly."

Brice reached for Brooke, but she stepped back out of his reach. "I'm in control," she stated emphatically.

"Yes, ma'am."

Brooke reached behind her and lowered her zipper. It was a feat Brice always found fascinating to watch when all she had to do was ask for his help. The dress fell to the floor, revealing the black lace bra and panty set she wore beneath it. "When does the game start again?"

"Wh-what?" Brice had lost his ability to think. He'd seen Brooke in similar things but this was different. Her erect nipples were peeking out through two holes in the bra that were clearly made for that purpose. From his vantage point, he could see the panties were crotchless.

Brice was harder than he'd ever been and it took everything in his power not to take her where she stood. "My goodness, baby."

"When does the game start?" she repeated. Brice could hear the humor in her voice.

"What game?"

"Good answer. Take off your shirt," she ordered, and he quickly obliged. "Shorts next, please. I want to see it."

Brice held her desire-filled gaze as he followed her instructions. He lowered his shorts to his thighs while he remained seated and his shaft made its grand entrance. A slow wicked smile spread across Brooke's face and the anticipation for what was about to happen had Brice silently praying for a less horny teenager-like response and a more controlled man-type one. He soon found that that wasn't at all what Brooke wanted.

Brooke dropped to her knees, gripped his thighs with both hands and parted his knees. "Oh damn..."

Brooke used her nose and closed mouth to play with his substantial erection. Brice's mind was racing; she was driv-

ing him crazy. While Brice loved what she was doing, he wanted to be inside of her mouth. He reached for her head, only to have his hands swatted away. "I'm in control."

"But, baby..."

"But what?" Brooke asked before her tongue began circling his shaft from the base to the tip. After several passes, Brice moaned Brooke's name and he knew how desperate he must've sounded but he didn't care. It must have been some type of trigger because Brooke took him in her mouth. She sucked and pulled on him as if she was determined to relieve him of some sweet elixir.

Brice was lost in the moment. He buried his hands in her hair and his hips matched her stroke. All he could think about was how much he loved and needed her. Brooke lifted her eyes as she caught him staring down at her. She released him, kissed her way up his stomach to his chest, following the fine line of hair. Brooke straddled Brice, lowering herself onto his sex until he was deep inside of her. Brice was thankful Brooke was on the Pill because if he had to stop and go find a condom he just knew his head would explode.

Brooke gazed into his eyes, whispering how much she loved him. She brought her knees in slightly, gripped the back of the sofa and rode him like she was on a horse in the Kentucky Derby. Brice's hands cupped Brooke's behind and he took her nipples into his mouth. He sucked and pulled on them hard just the way he knew she liked it. Her moans of satisfaction, orgasms and declarations of love ignited uncontrollable passion.

When Brooke's walls started to grip him with each thrust, Brice found himself thinking about math equations, chess moves, anything he could think of to keep him from reaching completion before Brooke. The two orgasms she'd already experienced were clearly the ap-

petizers for the meal she was after. Soon, he could no longer distract himself.

"Brooke...baby..." Brice yelled as he exploded.

"Yes...baby...yes," she screamed, having reached completion with him, collapsing into his arms.

Brice's eyes popped open and he sprang forward, releasing a string of profanity. He saw that the game had started but he looked down at his erection that needed to be handled first. "Damn, so much for not acting like a horny teenager. Back in a little bit, bro. Right after a long cold-ass shower," he explained to the TV.

He walked into the small three-quarter bathroom, stripped and walked under the overhead spray, hoping the cool water would calm his raging desire that thoughts of Brooke had invoked. Unfortunately, it only suppressed his passion, not quelling it. He decided there was only one way to do that; only he had no idea how he was going to make that happen.

Chapter 6

Three days had passed since Brooke finally accepted the fact that her life as Brice Kingsley's wife was over. There would be no more long walks in the park, getting lost in museums for hours on the weekends, intimate dinners or him loving her…making love to her. She missed his touch desperately. Brooke found herself struggling with how to keep her emotions in check whenever Brice was around. He, on the other hand, had clearly moved on. The few times she'd seen him over the last few days, he was nothing but professional and extremely polite. It was making her nuts.

Brooke was staring down at the spreadsheet she had been trying to make sense of for the last hour when she felt a tap on her shoulder. "Excuse me, Brooke."

She flinched and looked up. "Damon, you startled me."

"Sorry. I called your name twice. You must have really been concentrating on those numbers. Find anything interesting?"

I was concentrating all right, only on the wrong things.
"Not at all. What did you need?"

"I just want you to know I'm going to take the final first-quarter summaries up to Mr. Kingsley for review."

Brooke finally noticed the red folder he held in his hand. She rose from the chair, slipped her feet back into the red Prada shoes she'd paired with a red-and-white print short-sleeve dress and presented her palm. "I'll take them up."

Damon's eyes cut to Lori, and Brooke watched the corners of Lori's mouth rise as she sat back quietly in her chair. Brooke hadn't noticed the exchange. "Oh... Okay."

"You want to check your makeup too?" Lori teased.

"Don't be silly." Brooke walked toward the door.

"By the way, you have a couple of messages here—" she held up two pink notes "—from some woman who refused to leave her name."

Brooke frowned. "What?"

"She said, you'll know who it is."

Brooke walked back over to the conference table and looked at the messages. She read the number, recognizing it instantly. "Nope, I have no idea who this is," she lied, hoping her face wasn't as red as her outfit.

"What do you want me to do about them?"

"Trash them." Brooke walked out of the conference room. She was curious but Brooke didn't have the strength or the inclination to deal with old demons when she was still fighting present-day ones.

Brooke took the elevator up two floors and walked down the hall to Brice's office, passing several curious onlookers; she smiled and acknowledged their interest. Brooke reached Brice's open door and stopped. She didn't want to interrupt the friendly exchange he and Amy were having. What she really wanted to do was run and hide. Brooke knew if Brice ended their conversation the same way he used to end his conversations with her—with a passionate and often handsy kiss—she'd lose it; but for some reason, she couldn't turn away.

"Brooke... Brooke Kingsley?"

Brooke turn toward the sound of her name and smiled. China Kingsley, her soon-to-be ex-sister-in-law, was standing there wearing a straight blue dress with a white collar, rubbing her large expanded stomach with her right hand, looking as beautiful as ever. Pregnancy certainly agreed with her. It was just what she needed to break away from her obsession with Amy and Brice. Although, the last time Brooke had seen China, it helped her make the decision that changed everything.

China pulled Brooke into her arms. "I'm so happy to see you," she stated, smiling.

"Me too. You look amazing."

China gave a nonchalant wave. "Thanks, but I feel like a cow." Both women giggled as they moved to a small waiting area and sat down. "You look great yourself, but you could stand to gain some weight."

Another unwelcome gift from MS. "I know and I've tried. You're due pretty soon, right?" Brooke questioned, changing the subject.

"Yep, in about a week and half." China looked down and placed her hands on her belly. "I can't wait to meet this little stranger."

"I'm sure. You still don't know if it's a girl or boy?"

"Nope." A wide excited smile spread across China's face. "Although, Alexander seems to think it's a boy."

"Good morning, ladies," Amy greeted as she passed the two women heading toward the elevator. Brooke plastered on a fake smile and gave a quick nod to Brice's assistant as she walked into the waiting elevator.

China's forehead creased. "You're still not worried about Amy and Brice, are you?"

Brooke shrugged and shook her head. "Don't be silly.

Brice can do what or whomever he wants. It's no longer my business."

China folded her arms across her chest and gave Brooke the side-eye. "Oh, really?"

"Yes, really. We signed the divorce papers Monday," she informed her.

China adjusted herself in the seat. "I heard but that's just paperwork. I know it's none of my business—"

"But—"

"But whatever it is that made you run, you can talk to me about it. No matter what some piece of paper signed by any judge may say one day—" China reached over and squeezed Brooke's hand "—you'll always be family to me."

Brooke fought back tears. Having a family that loved and wanted her was all she'd ever really wanted and she thought she'd finally found one. Brooke often wondered about the teenage mother that had dropped her off at a fire station when she was four years old. She could never bring herself to try and find her. As a kid, Brooke figured, why should she? Brooke thought she would have her own family one day, which would make up for her loss. Too bad life had something else in mind. With a shy smile, she replied, "I'll remember that."

"There you are, Mrs. Kingsley," a gray-haired woman said as she approached with a worried look on her face.

"I'm fine, Mrs. Rogers," China replied, sounding somewhat put-off.

"Thank goodness. I leave to get you lunch and when I get back, no one knew where you'd gone," the flustered woman explained.

"And yet you still found me." China turned to Brooke. "Brooke Kingsley, meet Mrs. Rogers…my nanny."

"You've hired a nanny already?" She offered her hand, which the older woman shook and quickly dropped. "Please to meet you."

"No, I haven't hired a nanny for the baby yet." China shook her head and explained, "I'm still debating if I really need one since I'll be working from home for about a year or so."

"A year, wow, that's nice. So, what gives?" Her eyes shifted to the woman who was hovering over their shoulders.

"My husband, the whole family for that matter, felt it was best that I have my own Mary Poppins this last month or so."

Brooke giggled. "Why? Is everything all right?"

"Everything is fine. Everyone's just being extra careful."

Brooke opened her mouth slightly and nodded. "First grandbaby."

"Second."

"Second?" Brooke frowned.

"Did you hear that KJ and Mia got married?"

"I saw that online. I knew who she was but we never met."

"KJ adopted Mia's four-year-old son. Colby James Kingsley is Victoria's first heir and she's ecstatic. Victoria's already talking to a specialist to ensure he has everything he needs to continue to thrive."

"Thrive?"

"Yes, Colby has Down syndrome," China informed her.

"Wow, I had no idea."

China rubbed her belly. "Nothing but the best for the Kingsleys, and I'm not just talking about resources. You should keep that in mind."

"Excuse me, Mrs. Kingsley—"

China held up her hand, stopping the coming lecture. "I better get back before Alex sends out security to find us, if you don't mind giving me a little push while Mrs. Rogers pulls."

Brooke laughed. "Sure." After helping her friend up,

she gave her a hug and watched as she was escorted to the elevator, feeling envious of China's happiness.

Brooke walked back to Brice's office and stood in the doorway. She watched him studying a document as understanding dawned on his face and he nodded slowly. That was one of the things she loved most about Brice; he was thoughtful in everything he did.

Brooke knocked on the door and Brice looked up from his papers. "May I come in?"

"Sure," he replied, placing his document down on the desk, and standing to greet Brooke.

She entered the office, raising the folder she held. "I have the first-quarter summaries and our recommendations for your review."

"Great." He accepted the folder. "How do we look?"

"Nearly perfect…as usual. Please sit down. There are a couple of things highlighted."

Brice complied and started reading through the papers. "I came by a few moments ago, but Amy was here and I didn't want to interrupt. It looked pretty intense." *Really, Brooke, can you be any more obvious?* Brice kept his eyes on the report. "You've been really busy lately. I haven't seen much of you." Brooke ran her left index finger along the edge of his desk.

Brice looked up and said, "These recommendations are good. I'll talk to Alexander about them this afternoon. Great job, as always." His eyes dropped back down to the page.

For a moment, Brooke didn't know what to say. She realized Brice hadn't heard a word she'd said, and she felt like she was being dismissed. "Thanks, I'll tell my team." Brooke turned to leave.

"There's nothing going on between me and Amy." Brooke turned to meet his stare. "Not that my personal life is any of your business anymore. But I wanted you to know."

Brooke folded her arms and stared down at him. Her heart skipped several beats and she only hoped her foolish joy wasn't written all over her face. "I guess she's always been a sore spot for me."

"Unnecessarily." Brice stared up at her. "Amy has a thing for my cousin Travis, and besides, she has never been the one I wanted." The expression on his face was unreadable.

Brooke lowered her eyes and moved and stood behind his vertical desk. "I hear these things are good for your posture."

"They are." He turned in his chair and watched as she examined the desk.

"It's adjustable too, right?" Brice nodded. "It's just when you sent my copies of the divorce papers to the hotel the same day I signed them, I—"

"What are you talking about?" Brice opened his desk drawer and pulled out a large manila envelope. "Here are the papers. I haven't had a chance to do anything with them yet, and *I* most certainly wouldn't send your copy to you through the mail. There's just something very undignified about ending things in such a manner."

Brooke knew what that dig was about and she couldn't really blame him, either. "I assumed the package I got came from you. I didn't even open it."

"You might want to, because whatever you received wasn't from me." Brice returned the envelope to his drawer. "I'll send them out as soon as our attorney returns. He's away on business."

Brooke pushed a wayward piece of hair out of her face and behind her ears. "No rush."

Brice tilted his head to the right and frowned. "You sure about that? I mean, you have started seeing someone."

Brooke's eyebrows came to attention "No, I haven't. What are you talking about?"

"So the guy who picked you up the other night, the same guy I saw you holding hands with in Paris, is not your new man?" His voice turned hard.

Brooke's heart and mind raced. Not because of Brice's unfounded accusations, but because he had followed her and she'd had no idea. "You came to Paris?" She moved away from his vertical desk and return to her previous spot.

Brice came from around his desk, closed his door and stood in front of Brooke. He stared down at her with his hands buried in his pockets.

"Yes, now answer my question," he demanded.

"No, Peter is not my new man," she stated.

"Then who the hell is he?"

Brooke raised her chin and pushed back her shoulders. She held his angry gaze and fed him his own words. "Not that my personal life is any of your business, but Peter is my foster brother. He's the eldest son of the last family that took me in while I was in high school. I told you about him…them, remember?" Brice gave a quick nod. "Happy now?"

"You have no idea," Brice replied, and his eyes darkened.

"I haven't broken my vows," she whispered.

"Neither have I," he stated, pulling Brooke into his arms. "Neither have I." Brice's eyes roamed her face and she knew he was looking for any sign of rejection. One he wouldn't see. Brooke made sure Brice understood that she wanted what he was offering. She placed her hands on his chest and parted her lips, then Brice captured Brooke's mouth in a mind-blowing passionate kiss.

Chapter 7

Brooke's words had snapped something inside of Brice and all the lonely days and nights he'd suffered without her and the crazy thought he'd had about Brooke being with another man disappeared. Brice suddenly didn't care if they were technically married or not. All he wanted to do in that moment was hold and kiss his wife. He was just hoping she wouldn't push him away. What Brice hadn't expected was for Brooke to respond to his kiss with just as much passion. Brooke's arms flew around his neck as she rose up on her tippy toes. They kissed as if they were providing each other with life-sustaining breaths.

When their lungs demanded air, Brice buried his hands in her hair, destroying her well-crafted bun. He wrapped her locks around his hand, gently pulling her head back, exposing her beautiful neck. He slid his lips, nose and tongue across her cheek and down her neck. When he heard her whimper and moan his name, Brice swept Brooke into his arms and out of her shoes. He carried her over to the couch, a new addition to his office that he'd initially hated, but was now very grateful to have.

Brice laid Brooke on the sofa and stood back admiring her beauty. He wasn't sure how far he should take things. He didn't have to decide. Brooke beckoned him forward with her left index finger. The corners of his mouth rose. Brooke sat up and raised her dress over her head, dropping it to the floor, offering a viewing of the black lace underwear she was wearing. Brice's erection was fighting against its confinement. "Damn..."

Brooke's eyes dropped to his crotch. She looked up at him and whispered, "Please, baby."

Brice unzipped his pants. "This might be quick."

"Quick has never been an issue with us," she reminded him, licking her lips.

"True, but it's been a while. Self-service activities can only take you so far," he explained.

"I agree, so stop talking."

Brice chuckled and removed his tie and shirt. His pants soon followed, joining her dress on the floor. He'd forgotten how impatient Brooke got when she wanted him. That feeling meant everything to him and he'd missed it. He removed the fine cover over her sex and pushed it into the sofa's cushions.

"I meant what I said. I haven't been with anyone since we got together but if you'd like me to use a condom—"

"I trust you. I haven't been with anyone else either and I'm still on the Pill."

He came down on top of her. "I—"

Brooke stopped his words from escaping with an explosive kiss as she captured his erection with her right hand, placing it at her entrance. Brice thrust forward and Brooke moaned in his mouth. Her wet, warm walls engulfed him and Brice's mind cleared. He captured her face in the palm of his hands and devoured her mouth. He pulled back, repeating that thrust motion two more times. Brice stared into Brooke's eyes and watched as tears formed. Before he could set the pace that he knew would please them both, there was a knock on the door and the doorknob turned.

"Ignore it…please," Brooke begged softly.

"Brice…" Alexander called out.

"I can't. If I don't answer, he'll use his key," he explained.

Brooke's eyes went wide. "Then answer him…quickly."

"Yeah?" Brice yelled out.

"What's up? Why is the door locked?"

"I'm busy."

"Busy? We have to leave in fifteen minutes for Austin. The chopper's on the way. Open up."

"I can't. I'm busy, A. I'll meet you on the helicopter pad."

Brice and Brooke stared at the door in silence. "A?"

"See you in fifteen minutes," Alexander replied. Brice could hear the annoyance in his brother's voice.

Brice rested his forehead on Brooke's. "Sorry about that, baby, and I'm *really* sorry about this." He grimaced as he slowly pulled out of her.

"No…"

"I'm sorry, sweetheart." Brice gave her a quick kiss on the lips. "I totally forgot about this trip."

Brice picked up his clothes and walked into the bathroom, leaving a very dissatisfied-looking Brooke lying on the sofa. He took the fastest and coldest shower he'd ever had. Brice changed into a fresh set of clothes he kept at the office. He returned to find that Brooke hadn't moved.

"Are you all right?" he asked, adjusting his tie. Brooke looked up at him expressionless, still wearing her bra but naked from the waist down. Brice's body started to stir, so he tried to focus on her face.

"Do you remember that candy commercial where a kid

asked an animal of some kind how many licks of a sucker it took to get to the candy or gum inside? I can't remember which one it was or the type of animal."

Brice wasn't sure where this was going but replied, "Yes, the animal was an owl and the candy was a Tootsie Pop."

Brooke's eyes bored into him. She sat up, exhaled and stood. Brooke removed her bra and dropped it on the couch. Brice fought his desire for the woman he loved and wanted more than anything; the woman he'd only briefly just been inside of, who was standing naked in front of him, looking very annoyed, as she said, "You and that kid have something in common now."

"What's that?"

"He knows how many licks it took to get to his treat and now you know how many strokes it took to lose yours. Not to mention how to piss off your wife."

Brice burst out laughing and Brooke shot him a dirty look. She turned toward the bathroom, only Brice stopped her. He pulled her back into his arms and kissed her. "I'm sorry. I'll make it up to you when I get back. I promise."

Brooke stuck out her lip like an angry child that'd been denied their favorite toy. "When's that?"

"Tomorrow evening. How about I take you to dinner? We should talk about what this means."

"Okay, but this is closure for the both of us."

"I'll call you when I get back," he said, ignoring her explanation for what had just happened. The fact that she called herself his wife was all the hope he needed. He gave her another quick kiss. "Take your time. I'll lock the door."

Brooke watched as Brice left the office. She walked into the bathroom and looked in the mirror. "Closure? What in the hell is wrong with you?" She walked into Brice's shower and raised her face to the spray, allowing the water to wash over her, hoping to erase the actions of the last several minutes. She could only hope the excuse she'd given Brice was real. Closure was something they both needed. Brooke knew she couldn't stay married to Brice; she also knew she was not ready to let him go, either. Maybe finding something in between would be possible, at least for a little while.

She stepped out of the shower, dried off and squeezed as much water as she could out of her hair before pulling it back into a tight bun. Brooke returned to the office and re-dressed; only she couldn't find her underwear. "Brice." She shook her head, figuring that he must have taken them with him. "Commando it is."

Brooke unlocked and opened the door to find Brice's executive assistant, sitting at her desk. She looked up, smiled and said, "Good afternoon, Mrs. Kingsley."

"Good afternoon," she replied, hoping her face wasn't as red as the apple the older woman was eating.

Brooke made her way to the elevator and back to her office. She walked in to find Lori and Damon eating lunch. Brooke returned to the chair she had abandoned nearly an hour earlier and picked up her purse. She tried to ignore the look that passed between Lori and Damon.

"Hungry?" Lori asked, snickering. "Care for a little lunch?"

"Sure, in a bit," Brooke replied as she started reapplying her makeup.

Lori sat back in her chair. "Has it started raining in the building?" She raised a single brow.

"What?" Brooke pulled out her eyeliner.

"It's beautiful outside but you return from upstairs with your hair wet sans makeup."

"I'm going to go…somewhere else," Damon said, walking out of the office, closing the door behind him.

Brooke was in no mood for the lecture she knew was

coming. She held up her right hand. "Don't say a word. Please."

"I just hope you know what you're doing," Lori replied. *Me too.*

Brice and Alexander sat back in the limousine as the driver made his way through the Austin traffic, heading toward the state capital. Brice was wishing they could have taken their helicopter from Houston straight to their destination. "We have a good—" Alexander checked his Rotonde De Cartier watch "—twenty minutes before we get to the capitol building where I'm sure we'll be riveted by all the politicians clamoring for our money and contract extensions. You have until then to tell me why you've barely said a word from the time we left the office until now. I assume it has something to do with why you were locked away in your office in the middle of the day. I'm guessing you were with Brooke."

Brice pushed out a breath and laid his head back against the seat. He knew better than to try to lie to his brother, and frankly, he really could use his advice right now. Brice sat up and angled his body slightly toward Alexander. "Brooke brought up the first-quarter summaries—"

"Really, how do they look?" Alexander's face lit up.

"They look great, only a couple of minor recommendations. Do you want to hear about the report or me having an incomplete sexual encounter with my wife? Excuse me, my soon-to-be ex-wife."

Alexander's jaw dropped. "Definitely the latter."

Even after he confessed everything in detail to his brother in the next few minutes, Brice still couldn't believe what had happened. After months of uncertainty with where things stood with Brooke, not to mention his conflicting feelings, Brice finally had her back. Or did he?

"You got off easy. Well, actually you didn't." Alexander smirked.

"Funny…"

"Seriously, most women would be furious."

"Brooke wasn't exactly happy."

"So, what now?"

Brice hands flew up and fell to his lap. "I have no idea. Brooke called it 'closure.'"

"What do you call it?" Alexander asked, reaching for a buzzing phone and silencing it.

"That's just it—I really don't know what it means. I still love and want her but…"

"But what?"

"I can't deal with the uncertainty," he admitted.

That was the first time Brice had put words to his thoughts of concern. Yes, he loved her and wanted his wife back, but he knew he wouldn't be able to handle it if she just up and left again, especially since he didn't understand why she'd left in the first place. Brooke was right; they needed to find closure if they were going to move forward, whether with or without each other.

Alexander nodded. "I get that, so allow me to give you some of your own advice."

The car's partition descended and the driver said, "Excuse me, sirs, we'll be at the capitol in five minutes."

"Thank you," Alexander replied. Alexander waited for the partition to close before he spoke.

"What's the advice?" Brice tapped his own Cartier watch. "The clock's ticking."

"Give her what she wants."

Brice turned in his seat to fully face forward. "I did. She's keeping her name and she got a nice settlement, even though she didn't want it."

"That's not what I mean." Alexander pulled out his

buzzing phone and read the screen. "Looks like Mother won't be joining us until tomorrow."

"What? I thought this was one of those receptions we just had to attend. A show of force, as she put it."

"That's what she said, so whatever has her detained must be important," Alexander concluded.

"It had better be. To think…" Brice knew he shouldn't finish his thought aloud.

"What, so you could have finished what you started with Brooke? Then what? You'd still be struggling with these unresolved feelings."

"Okay, big brother, let's hear your fortune-cookie words of wisdom. What should I give Brooke that I haven't already?" he asked.

"Closure."

"You're telling me to have sex with my wife." Brice frowned.

"No, actually, I think you should do just the opposite."

Brice's frown deepened. "Excuse me?"

"We both know how sex can complicate things when you're not sure where you stand with someone."

"It worked out well for you and China," he stated.

"Yeah, but I almost lost her and our baby in the process."

Brice could see the pain of that memory overtake his brother's face. "Yet, everything worked out quite nicely for you two."

The spark returned to Alexander's eyes. "And I want the same thing for you too, man. Just slow things down a bit and see if you can find out why she really left. We all know there had to be more to it than what she said. I saw you two together. The way she looked at you whenever you were around. She really loved you."

Brice simply nodded. He was experiencing too many emotions to speak.

"If I'm honest, I thought she might have fooled us all and was only after a big payday when you told me about Paris. But now, we know that wasn't what it appeared to be. I think there's more to the story than you know. I think you should find out what it is before you risk your heart any further. That's it. That's my fortune-cookie advice."

"Not bad. China would be proud. Speaking of which, how did you pull yourself away from her this late in the pregnancy?"

"She forced me to go. I think my hovering is driving her crazy. I'm only a forty-minute plane ride away."

"And how many times have you told yourself that?"

"Only about a hundred times...a minute."

"Thanks, man." Brice and Alexander bumped fists as the car came to a stop.

"Let's go see if Mother's political contributions have paid off. Time to renegotiate a few contracts. Ready for this?" Alexander pointed at the reporters waiting for their exit.

"Not as much is I'm ready for answers from Brooke," he proclaimed as he exited the car.

Chapter 8

"It's nearly six. Why don't we call it a day?" Brooke offered.

"You don't have to tell me twice," Lori replied, powering down her computer.

"Great. I can't move forward until we get feedback from Mr. Kingsley, anyway." Damon packed up his things. "I'll see you ladies tomorrow."

Damon walked out of the office and Brooke snickered. "I wonder who he's seeing tonight, the redhead or the blonde," Brooke speculated.

"Knowing Damon, both," Lori said, laughing.

"You're probably right." Brooke stood and her legs gave way, dropping her back down into her chair.

"You all right?"

"God don't like ugly," she said, trying to lighten the mood.

"I'm serious," Lori said, coming to stand next to Brooke.

"I'm fine. I've just been sitting too long." Lori's eyes

bored into Brooke. "Really, they aren't numb, just asleep." *My left hand is another issue and so is the pain in my lower back and legs.*

"If you say so. Your car is downstairs whenever you're ready to go."

"Thanks, Lori." Brooke smiled, gritting her teeth through the pain, determined to keep her friend from worrying.

"I'll see you tomorrow."

Brooke sat and used her right hand to massage her left. She kicked off her shoes and started slowly rotating her legs as if she was riding a bike. After several minutes, Brooke tried to relax as she reached for her phone. She hit two numbers and waited for the call to connect. While Brooke waited, she fought her fear and removed a medicine bottle from her bag, pulled out a pain pill and swallowed it down with water from her glass that sat on the table.

"It's about time you called me. I was worried. How are you?"

"I'm fine, but I need your help, Lisa."

Lisa Barrington had been Brooke's best friend since they'd met in one of the many group homes where she'd stayed. After graduating high school, Brooke and Lisa put themselves through college by working for the same high-end escort service. An escort service that only offered companionship.

"What's up? How is your health?"

"Fine, thanks for asking. You'll never guess who's been calling and leaving me messages." Brooke took another sip from her glass.

"Who?" Lisa's voice rose an octave. Brooke knew she was expecting her to dish about Brice. She was always trying to convince her to tell her everything.

"Shannon Rivers, and I have no idea what she could want."

"Knowing that cow, she either wants money or more money. You married into a very wealthy family," Lisa explained nonchalantly.

"Well—"

"What's she threatening you with?"

"Threatening me... She hasn't."

"Hmm..."

"What... What is it?" Brooke could feel the meds starting to work; her pain was easing.

"Blackmailing people for money seems to be her new business plan."

"Well, she doesn't have anything to hold over me," Brooke insisted, trying to convince herself and her friend that was true. The idea that Shannon was coming for her again scared the hell out of her.

"I realize that, but it's never stopped her before."

Brooke heard something strange in her friend's voice. "What did she do to you?"

"Me? Nothing, but she's hurt others."

"I guess she's still scared of you. She remembers that butt whipping you put on her," Brooke reminded Lisa, and both women laughed.

"That's really strange. The way I understand it, she usually sends something cryptic before she makes direct contact."

"Like what?"

"A bouquet of dead roses, cookies made with salt instead of sugar—"

"Seriously, Lisa?"

"Stupid, I know. You sure she didn't send you anything to announce her presence?"

Brooke's forehead creased and she shook her head slowly. "No... I don't think so. Wait..."

"What?"

"I got a package a few days ago, but I never opened it. I

thought it was something from Brice. But given her phone calls and what you've said it's probably safe to assume it's something from her." Brooke's curiosity was piqued.

"Well, maybe you should see what she wants. In the meantime, what's going on between you and Brice?"

"You won't believe me if I told you."

"Try me."

Brooke spent the next fifteen minutes explaining her close encounter with Brice. "Lisa… Lisa, you still there?"

"I'm still here. I'm just shocked."

"Me too. I can't believe I did it."

"Oh, I can believe you did it. What I can't believe is that you let him go without finishing," she said, laughing.

Brooke giggled. "Only you would think about that right now."

"Seriously, what's going on with you? What do you want to happen with Brice?"

Brooke's heart felt like someone had reached in her chest and started performing CPR. "What I want I can't have. We all can't be like you."

"Oh, but you are. Brice may not have been a former client you married, but he is the love of your life and you can keep him if you really want him. Just tell Brice about the MS and your past. If he doesn't accept you, then to hell with him. It's not like you ever had sex with any of your clients."

"That's just it. He probably would stay with me for the wrong reasons."

"Don't you think that's his choice to make?"

Brooke rubbed her temples. "You sound just like Peter."

"Great minds think alike."

"Yeah… Yeah. I have to go check my mail. I'll call you about Shannon as soon as I know something." Brooke rose slowly from her seat.

"Let me know if you need anything. You have family,

you know. Eddie and I are only a plane ride away," Lisa
reminded Brooke, her voice suddenly serious.

"I know. Love you," Brooke replied, as memories of the
crazy antics the two of them had shared over the years together flooded her mind.

"Love you too."

Brooke disconnected and dropped the phone in her
purse. She slowly made her way down to her waiting car.
When she arrived back at the hotel, Brooke had the driver
drop her off at the side-street entrance; it was a shorter
walk to the elevator. Once Brooke got upstairs into her
suite, she went to her bedroom closet, opened the safe and
removed the manila envelope. Feeling a little lightheaded,
Brooke went and sat on her king-size bed. She opened the
sealed envelope and dropped the contents onto the bed.

"My God." She brought her right hand to her mouth
and the left landed on her stomach. She ran to the bathroom on wobbly legs, dropped to her knees—having lost
her shoes along the way—and emptied what little she had
in her stomach into the porcelain bowl. After a couple of
more deposits, Brooke got to her feet and moved to the sink
where she brushed her teeth and washed her face. She tim-
idly walked back to the bedroom and looked down at the
obviously doctored photos of herself in sexually explicit
positions with both men and women.

In addition to the disgusting photos, there was another
smaller envelope that Brooke was cautious about opening.
With a shaking hand, Brooke picked up the envelope and
broke the seal. Inside was a small card with numbers on it
and several other affidavits, which claimed Brooke was a
willing and well-paid participant in this, which was a lie.

Brooke's whole body started to shake as tears welled
in her eyes. She knew what needed to be done, but she
also knew she wouldn't be able to make her mind or body
work together much longer. "What a time to have an MS

flare-up." Brooke sat on the bed and reached for the medicine bottles that sat on her nightstand. After taking her
pills, she pulled her dress over her head, dropping it to
the floor. Brooke climbed under the covers and waited
for the darkness to take her, thinking about seeing Brice
when she woke up.

Brice sat in the restaurant of the Hilton Austin Hotel
where he had stayed the night. A plate with a steak and
eggs sat in front of him and all he could think about was
Brooke. He was actually wondering what she was having
for breakfast. "Get a grip, man," he mumbled, adjusting
his tie, feeling uncomfortable.

"What was that, Brice, darling?" Victoria asked as she
took the seat across from him.

Brice rose from his chair quickly. "Sorry, Mother. I
didn't see you come in."

"I can see that… Sit. What has you so deep in thought?"
she asked, placing a napkin in her lap.

"Don't you look beautiful in your red power suit," he
said, smiling down at her and hoping to distract her from
a question he wasn't ready to answer.

"Thank you, son."

"Yes, little brother," Alexander said as he walked up to
the table. He took the empty seat between the two. "Tell
us what's on your mind."

Brice picked up his fork and knife and cut into his steak.
"I was just thinking about how good this looks." He took
a bite of his food.

"Sure you were." Alexander gestured for the waiter to
come forward. "Mother…" Alexander prompted.

"Oh, no, I've eaten already," she informed her eldest
son.

"I'll have the same thing that my brother is having."

"Right away, sir."

"How about we go over the first-quarter summaries from the audit before we're stuck behind closed doors for the next few hours? I can't believe we're here trying to hammer out a new deal with the same government that's trying to bring us down," Victoria complained, reaching for a glass of orange juice.

"Neither can I," Brice said, reaching for his coffee cup.

"No concessions on our fees this time, either," Alexander expressed firmly.

"Keeping our per barrel rates flat for the last three years is enough. How much did we save the government on our last contract, Brice?" Victoria asked.

Brice's thoughts were back on Brooke, so he wasn't sure if he'd heard his mother's question correctly, but he had to hope he did because if he gave her the wrong answer Alexander would certainly know why.

"One point eight billion dollars," Brice said.

"Yet, they can't control all their regulatory agencies from coming after us on bogus claims." Victoria took another sip from her glass.

The waiter returned with Alexander's breakfast and placed it in front of him. "Thanks. Can I have some steak sauce, please?"

"Right away, sir."

"Yeah, and you know they're going to come out of the box with that savings request too." Alexander accepted the sauce from the waiter.

"They can always ask, son."

Brice finished off his food and pushed his plate forward. "You're right about that, Mother. Just because you want something doesn't mean you should have it or will receive it."

Brooke slowly opened her eyes. She stretched her arms out to her side and flexed her feet. Brooke took a deep breath and released it slowly. She was pain-free and she knew she'd be seeing Brice tonight and that made her smile, until she remembered the reason this particular flare-up had been so difficult to manage. She looked over and saw the evidence of her distress lying in the same area of her bed where she'd left it.

She sat up and reached for the photos. Brooke grimaced and her heart raced as she forced herself to view each disgusting picture, one after the other. "How could they?" Brooke collected all the doctored photos and the fake affidavits and returned them to their original envelope. "I'm not going to let you get away with this."

Brooke reached for her phone and dialed the one person she knew who could help her fix this mess without involving Brice and the media. Unfortunately, her call went to voice mail, so she sent a brief text requesting a meeting as soon as possible. While she waited for a reply, Brooke showered and got dressed for work—a simple black suit and white blouse seemed appropriate. She lightly made up her face, stepped into her shoes and went in search of her purse when her cell phone beeped. Brooke picked up her phone and read the message.

I'll arrive in Houston at four. I'll see you at five.

She immediately texted back her appreciation and thanks. Feeling a small sense of relief, and even a little brave by her decision, Brooke called Shannon.

"Brooke Kingsley, what a pleasant surprise."

"Cut the crap, Shannon. What do you want and why did you make all those disgusting photos you sent to me?"

"I assure you I don't know what you're talking about, but why don't we meet downstairs in your hotel's restaurant for breakfast? We can discuss it in, say, fifteen minutes. See you soon," Shannon stated before disconnecting the call.

Brooke texted Damon and Lori that she would be late before putting the envelope from Shannon into her briefcase. She decided to wait for Shannon downstairs, so she picked up her purse and briefcase and made her way down to the restaurant. To her surprise, Shannon was already sitting in a two-person booth in the front of a set of sliding glass windows, seemingly enjoying a glass of orange juice from a champagne glass. Brooke knew better and assumed the glass held more than just orange juice. Brooke took a deep breath, releasing it slowly with each step she made toward Shannon's table.

"May I help you, Mrs. Kingsley?" a young woman wearing a black-and-white uniform asked, her eagerness to help on full display.

"No, thank you." Brooke glared across the room at the beautiful dark-haired woman dressed in a black-and-red dress and a pair of black red-bottomed shoes. Too bad Shannon's black heart and mean spirit overshadowed her beauty. Shannon offered her a lopsided grin. "I see my party."

Brooke approached Shannon's table, trying to muster all her strength and courage. *You got this. Just say what you need to and go.*

"Brooke Kingsley, or is it back to Smith now? It doesn't matter. Please." She gestured with her right hand for Brooke to sit in the chair across from her. "Join me."

"That won't be necessary. I'm just here to tell you I'm not playing games with you. Leave me the hell alone and whatever it is you want, the answer is no." Brooke stared down at Shannon.

"Making a scene in a public restaurant seems counterintuitive to your family's desire to keep their private lives private, don't you think?" Shannon took a sip from her glass.

Brooke looked over her shoulder and found that she had in fact gained the attention of several patrons. She smiled and nodded as she took a seat.

"Now that you've gotten that off your chest—" Shannon waved over the waiter "—we're ready to order and please bring my friend here a mimosa."

Brooke held up her right hand. "No, thank you. I'm not hungry. I'll just have coffee."

"Well, I am. I'll have the Spanish omelet."

"I'll get that right away." The waiter turned and left.

Shannon slid a white envelope that Brooke hadn't noticed across the table to her. "Open it."

"More lies?" Brooke picked up the envelope and reluctantly opened it and pulled out the document. As she read and flipped through the pages, all her bravado disappeared. The waiter returned with Brooke's coffee.

"I think my friend will have that mimosa now."

Brooke nodded her agreement. "What do you want?"

Chapter 9

"Don't be ridiculous, son. We're Kingsleys. We always get what we want, because what we want is what's best for our family's business. We've all worked really hard to ensure our continued success and we won't let any nonsense interfere with that."

"Not everything's about business, Mother," Alexander replied, shaking his head.

"That's where you're wrong, son. Everything is about business, be it professional or personal. You children are led by your emotions versus your head when it comes to your personal lives." Victoria picked up the glass of water in front of her and took a drink. "If you were more strategic and less reactive in everything you do, you'd be surprised by just how far you can go in getting *whatever* you want."

Brice and Alexander looked at each other; their brows knitted. "Wow. Who are you and what *have* you done with our mother?" Alexander questioned.

"What's wrong with you two?" Victoria asked, her eyes shifting between her two sons.

"That was actually pretty poignant advice," Alexander complimented.

"Thoughtful too," Brice offered, realizing his mother was right. He'd been too emotional in his efforts to get Brooke back. It was time to try a new approach. Brice needed to be methodical in trying to get Brooke back, much like his methods of conducting business.

Victoria rolled her eyes skyward and gave them a nonchalant wave. "Of course, I'm right."

"And she's back," Alexander said, laughing.

"If you two are finished—" Victoria rose from her seat "—I'd like to head to the capitol."

Brice looked down at Alexander's half-eaten plate. "Can Alexander finish his breakfast?"

"I'm good," Alexander said, wiping his mouth with his napkin before dropping it on the table. "The sooner we get this day started, the sooner we can get back home."

"Only if we have the deal we want, understand?" Victoria instructed.

Brice stood. "Yes, of course. But it may take more than one meeting to accomplish that, Mother."

Victoria narrowed her eyes. "The only other meeting I'm willing to attend with these people is the contract signing…period!"

"Mother, you know it usually takes more than one meeting with the principals to finalize a deal," Alexander reminded.

"That's why I have assistant principals in you two. We're an independent company that's rich and powerful enough to walk away from any deal." Victoria reached into her bag and pulled out her sunglasses. "They need us more than we need them. So get the deal done on our terms and I'll happily sign it…only at my office. Let those bastards come to me."

"Yes, ma'am." Brice smiled. He always admired how strong and steadfast his mother was when it came to business.

"Shall we?" Alexander offered their mother his arm.

Brice signed the check and dropped a hundred-dollar bill down on the table. He smirked at the memory of Brooke informing him, sometime after they'd met, of how important it was to always tip service people extremely well. Not that he hadn't always done so, but her passionate pleas for those less fortunate had always made him proud.

"Coming, son?"

"Absolutely." Brice couldn't wait to get this day done so he could get back to Brooke. They had some serious unfinished business he had every intention of finishing, in spite of his brother's advice. He wanted his wife.

Brooke sat in silence as she finished off her second mimosa, trying to find the courage to continue and sit there watching Shannon gloat. Even though the photos were fakes and the so-called affidavits were lies, the other item inside this new envelope was real. Brooke looked down at it. "Where did you get this?"

"You're not the only one who dated powerful men, you know. Except I kept in touch with those relationships in case I ever needed favors."

Brooke's nostrils flared. "Favor? You mean blackmail."

China shrugged. "To-may-to…to-mah-to."

"Your omelet, ma'am." The waiter placed the plate in front of Shannon and turned his attention toward Brooke. "Are you sure you don't want anything?"

Brooke wanted to say no, but now that she'd had two drinks she knew she needed to put something in her stomach. "I think I will have a little something. How about scrambled eggs and toast?"

"Right away." The waiter turned and walked away.

"What do you want?" Brooke asked, glaring at Shannon.

"I need your help and this time I won't take no for an answer. I have a partner now that's not nearly as understanding as I am."

"What do you mean, you have a partner? Since when and who is it?"

"That's none of your concern. Let's just say it's someone who helped me expand my business and taught me the benefit of keeping an eye on old employees such as yourself. You never know when you may need to reach out for a favor or two."

A chill ran down Brooke's spine. "What kind of favor?"

A slow wicked smile crawled across Shannon's face. "One that should be very easy for you to accomplish."

To find peace of mind for herself and her family, Brooke would do whatever she had to, including giving up every dime she had. Brooke knew this had to be about money since the last time they spoke that was what she wanted.

"How much is truth and silence going for these days?" Before Shannon could answer, the waiter returned with Brooke's plate of food. "Thank you."

Shannon laughed as she took a drink from her cup.

"So…" Brooke lightly buttered her toast before she took a bite. She needed to keep herself settled.

"We don't want *your* money." Shannon finished off her omelet.

"What exactly does that mean?" Brooke ate her eggs, thankful for having something in her stomach other than orange juice and champagne.

"Talk about a small world. It seems you and my partner have something in common."

"What?" Brooke's forehead creased.

Shannon used her napkin and wiped her mouth. "History. More precisely, a history with someone that my partner and I need your help with in getting something back that belongs to him...plus a little interest."

"Stop with all the games. What is it that you want?"

Shannon sucked her teeth. "You've never been any fun. In the envelope with the affidavits there was a business card with the name of a bank and a bank account number," she started to explain. "Did you see it?"

"Yes."

"Good." Shannon reached in her purse that was hanging on the back of her chair and pulled out another envelope and handed it to Brooke.

"What's this?"

"Inside, you'll find a list of bank accounts—"

"Bank accounts?" Brooke frowned. "I thought you didn't want my money."

"We don't and if you'd stop interrupting me, I can lay out your assignment."

Brooke's head jerked. "My assignment?" Shannon sat back and folded her arms. "Sorry. Continue."

"The account number on the card we gave you belongs to Victoria Kingsley."

"What?" Brooke's brow puckered; she knew she must have heard wrong.

"Imagine my surprise when one Sunday afternoon, while me and my partner were in bed, sharing old life stories, I find out that your mother-in-law stole a great deal of money from him." Shannon placed her right hand over her heart as if she was about to recite the Pledge of Allegiance. "Now I wouldn't be a good partner, not to mention lover, if I didn't I share our history, Brooke. We want the money back, along with the appropriate amount of interest."

"I don't believe you." Brooke shook her head.

"I don't give a damn what you believe," Shannon said through gritted teeth. "You're going to pull out every dime and split it evenly over all of those accounts."

"Look, I just got my divorce settlement. Well, I'll have it real soon and it's yours. Every dime. Please just leave the Kingsleys alone." Brooke's heart was racing and the dull ache in her lower back now felt like sharp needles being stabbed slowly into her spine.

"Isn't that sweet? You'll need that money, because you're going to have to disappear once the job is done."

"What?"

Shannon glared at Brooke. "Don't you know anything? The Kingsleys are going to be after blood when they find out what you've done." Shannon leaned forward and whispered, "There're only a handful of people who know about that particular account, so trust me, Victoria will figure it out sooner or later. Anyway, your settlement is nowhere near the seventy million in that account."

Brooke's head started to spin. "Seventy million...dollars?"

"Yes, and we want every single dime too."

Brooke fought back tears and raised her nose in the air. "What's to stop me from going to the Kingsleys right now and telling them everything?"

"Because you're not that brave or that stupid. You know we will release all those photos, plus a few more I didn't send you, along with the statements from every man and woman you slept with."

"That's a lie and you know it." Brooke slammed her palm against the table.

Shannon released an audible sigh. "Don't you know a scandalous lie that sells papers or garners clicks and likes is more believable than the truth? Add that little bit of truthful information—" Shannon pointed to the envelope that now lay on the table next to Brooke's water glass "—and the story will go viral in a matter of hours, humiliating the Kingsleys, especially your soon-to-be ex-husband, and seriously shaking the confidence of all their business associates. They're already under attack by the government. This will just add fuel to the already raging fire around them. I can see the headlines now. *Former Sex Worker Marries a Kingsley* or better yet, *Brooke Kingsley Trades Sex for Contracts.* I'm sure that would do wonders for your own business too. How many of your wealthy clients will want to entrust their interests to you after all that?"

Brooke felt sick. She knew everything Shannon said was correct. By the time she cleared her name, the damage would be done. Then she heard Lisa's voice in her head: *You're not in this alone.* Brooke remembered that she too had powerful people in her life that could help. She put the envelope in her purse and stood. She leaned forward, slightly gripping the table. Shannon frowned at her movement.

"Thank you for the breakfast. I assume you'll be taking care of the bill. As for your request, my answer is no."

"No?" Shannon expression hardened.

"N.O. I won't hurt my family…ever!" Brooke declared.

"We'll see about that," Shannon promised.

Brooke knew it wouldn't be that easy. She was declaring war. "Yes, we will." She picked up her briefcase, leaving the list of accounts on the table, and walked out of the restaurant to her waiting car.

Chapter 10

Brooke spent the painful ride to her office reading and rereading the one piece of incriminating evidence from her past that Shannon actually had. She'd thought that, between completing the deferred adjudication process and having her record sealed and legally changing her name, that this part of her past was dead and buried. Yet somehow Shannon managed to resurrect one of the worst times in her life to use it against her. Why was she surprised? Brooke was so deep in thought she hadn't realized the car had come to a stop. Brooke jumped when the door opened.

"Mrs. Kingsley." The driver offered Brooke his hand.

"Thank you." Brooke grabbed her things, accepted the driver's assistance and stepped gingerly out of the car.

"Shall I be here the same time as always?"

"Yes, please," she answered through gritted teeth.

Brooke made her way inside the building and up to her office, feeling each painful step she took. She walked in and reached for the closest chair where she slowly sat down.

"Good morning," Damon said, frowning.

"Good morning, boss," Lori greeted her, with a worried look on her face. "What's wrong?"

Brooke looked up at her concerned friend with every intention of reassuring her that she was fine but words failed. The tears she'd been fighting fell and she released a loud, painful moan.

Lori ran to close the door before returning to Brooke's side. "Are you in pain?"

Brooke nodded. Between her back and leg pain, not to mention her heart breaking at the idea of hurting the Kingsleys, Brooke wasn't sure what hurt more. "P-pills," she whispered.

Lori reached into Brooke's purse and pulled out her medicine. She gestured for Damon to toss her one of the water bottles that sat in the middle of the conference table. "Here you go." Brooke took the pills and finished off half the water bottle.

"Should we call a doctor or something?" Damon asked.

"No," Brooke whispered. "I'll be fine in a few minutes."

"Let's help her over to the sofa," Lori instructed Damon.

Brooke was grateful for the offer of help but refused. She slowly walked the few feet and sat down. "Sorry, guys, it looks like I'll be working from this spot today." She offered up a small smile.

"Would you like for us to take you back to the hotel?" Damon asked.

"Of course not. I'll be fine in about an hour." Brooke lay down on her side. "Just go back to work."

Lori and Damon stared at her. "Okay, if you need something just call out," Lori said.

Brooke nodded, closed her eyes and waited for the pain to subside.

"I can't believe Mom bailed on the final stage of these negotiations," Brice said, reaching across the conference table to retrieve a cookie from the snack tray that had been placed in the middle of it.

"I don't know why not. You know Mom has a short attention span these days when it comes to nuances of the deal. Let's just make this break quick so we can get this done," Alexander reminded Brice, keeping his eyes on his cell phone. "China wants me to invite you over for dinner tonight."

"I'm hoping I'll have other plans." Brice pulled out his phone. "Dammit."

"What?"

"I texted Brooke about dinner tonight but she hasn't texted me back yet."

"How about you just give her a call?" Alexander suggested.

"I did and it went to voice mail, which is strange." Brice frowned.

"Why?"

"She never turns off her phone."

"Then call her at the office," Alexander recommended.

"Good idea." Brooke had Brice so twisted up in his feelings he couldn't think clearly.

Brice held the phone to his ear. "Well?" Alexander asked.

"They're getting her for me," Brice informed his curious brother, feeling both nervous and excited to hear Brooke's voice.

"Hi, Brice, sorry I missed your calls and texts. My phone needs to be charged," Brooke explained.

"Oh, okay." Brice stood and stepped away from the conference table. "Are you all right? You sound funny."

Brooke laughed and his heart skipped a beat. "Gee, thanks. I'm fine."

"Sorry. I was calling to see…umm…if you were available for dinner." Brice actually held his breath as he waited for Brooke's answer.

"I'd like that...very much." Brice pumped his fist in the air and a big smile crawled across his face. That was, until the next words fell from her lips. "But—"

"But..." Brice felt like he'd just been hit in the gut.

"It will need to be a late dinner—how's eight-thirty?"

Brice released a deep sigh and Brooke giggled. "Oh, sure. Cool. That's fine. I'll pick you up at your hotel."

"See you later, Brice."

"La-later." Brice stared down at his screen and watched Brooke's name disappear. He put his phone away and returned to the table to a confused-looking Alexander. "What?"

"What the hell was that? You sounded like a fifteen-year-old kid asking a girl out for the first time."

"Man, forget you," he snapped back, knowing his brother was right. But Brice had an idea of how he could get some of his cool points back. He pulled out his phone again and sent his assistant a text message.

"I hope you get it together before tonight." Alexander laughed.

"Whatever. Let's get this wrapped up. I want to get out of here on time."

"I bet you do. So I guess I should tell China, next time."

"Rain check." Brice stood and headed to the door. "I'll go get the suits back in here."

Brooke sat back in her chair, smiling down at the phone. "Sounds like you changed your mind about a few things," Lori deduced, her left eyebrow raised.

"It's just dinner."

"It's never just dinner," Lori teased.

"I can't believe I slept through most of the day," Brooke replied, changing the subject.

"Your pain meds are pretty heavy-duty."

Brooke nodded. "That's why I try not to have to take them." Then she remembered the reason she'd needed the help in the first place and frowned. Brooke checked the time on her computer. "You guys can cut out early. Get a jump start on the weekend."

"Seriously?" Damon's face lit up.

"Seriously! We're done with the first-quarter review and second-quarter material isn't going anywhere. We can get a fresh start on everything first thing Monday morning. Go. Get an early start on your Friday." Brooke gave a nonchalant wave.

"Cool. Friday night with my boys and Saturday with my girls," Damon informed.

"Boy, bye," Lori said, rolling her eyes. "So…" She gave Brooke the evil eye.

"So… What?"

"It's three forty-five and you're pushing us out. You got a hot date to get ready for or something? Oh, yeah, that's right, you do." Lori rested her hands on her hips. "I hope you know what you're doing."

"You don't have to worry about me. I'll be fine. Aren't you the one who's been telling me to come clean with Brice? What, have you changed your mind?"

"Of course not. I think he has a right to know about your MS. I'm just surprised you agree with me."

"Like I said, it's just dinner." *My MS is the least of my worries right now.* "Let's just say I'm keeping my options open right now."

Lori picked up her things. "You coming?"

"Not yet. Since I missed nearly a day's worth of work, the least I can do is catch up on my emails."

"Would you like for me to stay?"

Brooke smiled. "No, I appreciate the offer but I'm fine. Go enjoy your weekend."

"I will." Lori wiggled her eyebrows as she walked out the door.

Brooke pulled the envelope that Shannon had given her out of her purse and removed the business card. She turned to the computer and searched for the bank statements associated with the account number on the card. "Oh, wow." Brooke printed out copies of the statements. She knew it was time to find out who she was really dealing with, so she picked up her phone and dialed a reliable source for the information she needed.

It took Lisa less than an hour to reach out to several people from their past and gather all the intel she could, which she happily shared with her friend. Brooke sat behind her desk and waited for her guest to arrive. Soon there was a knock on the door and the knob turned. Brooke checked the time. "Right on time as always." She stood and plastered on a fake smile. *You can do this. Just tell the truth.* The door opened and Victoria entered the room. She wore a black Yves St. Laurent jumpsuit with a crystal trimmed peak lapel. Even when she was dressed casually, she looked regal.

"Brooke, dear, what has you in such a frenzy and why did I have to keep this meeting a secret?" she questioned, standing in the middle of the room.

Brooke came from around her desk. "Please have a seat and I'll explain everything."

Victoria placed her bag on the small glass coffee table before she sat on the sofa. Brooke sat in one of the chairs across from her.

"Well…"

"I… I'm not sure where to begin, Victoria."

"How about at the beginning?" Victoria sat back and crossed her legs as if she was expecting a great tale.

"Okay. My name is Smith. Well, it's not just Smith—It's Brooke Avery Smith."

"Aww, that explains it."

"Explains what?" Brooke frowned.

"There wasn't much to find on Brooke Smith other than a birth certificate, a stellar college record and your short work history. I just figured that was because you grew up in the foster care system," Victoria explained.

"You had me investigated?"

Victoria's forehead creased as if that was the most ridiculous question she'd ever heard. "Yes, of course, I had you investigated. Not only were you joining my company, you were working with my son. My handsome and extremely wealthy son."

"You were protecting your family like always," Brooke deduced, nodding slowly.

"Now what is it that I don't know about Brooke Avery?" Victoria raised her left eyebrow.

Brooke sat up straight in her chair, crossing her legs at her ankles, and placed her hands in her lap. "You already know I grew up in the foster care system after I was dropped off at a fire station with my birth certificate and twenty dollars pinned to my clothes—"

"Yes, you explained that when you and Brice started dating. You were four."

"Yes."

Victoria frowned. "I never understood how that could happen."

Brooke shrugged. "My birth mother was only fifteen when she had me and I guess after a few years of playing Mommy she'd had enough."

"That's not what I meant. I thought you could only leave a baby at the fire station."

"Oh, well, initially kids' ages weren't specified. She got lucky… I didn't. I lived with a couple of crappy foster families but because I stayed sick with asthma, nothing stuck. Then I was moved into a few different group homes, which were cool…for the most part, especially after I met my best friend Lisa. Then, my senior year in high school, I moved in with the Schultz family."

Victoria nodded. "Your last foster family."

"Yes, the Schultzes were wonderful. They're an older couple who were already well-off so they weren't in it for the check."

"That makes a difference," Victoria concluded.

"It does. Anyway, the summer after graduation, I left and moved in with Lisa."

"The one that's married to Eddie Barrington, the real-estate tycoon."

"Yes. To make money for school, we…" Feeling like her throat was on fire, Brooke rose from her chair and walked over to the small refrigerator and pulled out a bottle of water. "Care for anything?"

"No."

Brooke twisted off the cap and took a big gulp. She was trying to calm herself so she could get the next few words out of her mouth. She returned to her seat with the water bottle, placing it on the table.

"What did you do to make money, Brooke?" Victoria's face was expressionless.

"I went to work for a high-end escort service."

Chapter 11

Brice paced the VIP area of the airport while they waited to board. "What's going on? Why can't we wait on our own damn plane?"

Alexander sat back on the small low-backed leather sofa with his legs stretched out. "Did you not feel all that wind we drove through when we came in? Not to mention the rain."

"This dustup is nothing."

"Well, it's enough to keep us grounded for a few more minutes. Chill, you'll make your date."

Brice stopped and turned toward his brother. "You wouldn't be so nonchalant about things if China was in labor," he retorted, glaring down at his brother.

"True, I'd be acting as crazy as you, and we'd still be grounded."

Brice's shoulders dropped and he sat in the seat across from Alexander. "I know I'm tripping, but Brooke actually agreed to have dinner with me and she sounded excited. A little. I think."

Alexander smirked. "I get it. Hope can be a bitch."

"I know." Brice ran his hand under the bottom of his chin.

"Excuse me, sirs. I've been advised that we've been cleared to leave—"

"Excellent…" Brice popped to his feet.

"In about an hour," the attendant continued.

Brice's heart sank while Alexander clapped and laughed. "Thank you, miss," Brice said as the young woman smiled and left.

"Man, you popped up like a jack-in-the-box," Alexander teased.

"Whatever…" Brice started pacing the room again.

Alexander stood. "I told you, you're making me dizzy. Let's go to the bar across the way for a beer."

"Why, when we can have a beer here in the lounge?"

"Because we both could use the distraction. You from your date and me from how long I've been away from my wife. Besides, it's too quiet in here. We need noise."

"We better tell the attendant where we're going," Brice recommended. "We don't want to miss our place in line for takeoff."

"Good point. I'll be right back."

Brice thought his connection with Brooke in his office and her response to his request for a date meant there was still something very special between them. Brice had a feeling tonight would change things between him and Brooke forever.

"Did you hear what I said? I was a high-end escort, but I never had sex with any of my clients. No matter how hard they tried or how much money I was offered. I couldn't. I swear."

Victoria tilted her head slightly to the right and Brooke could feel her eyes bore into her. "How long were you an escort?"

"Eighteen months."

"I see. There has to be more to this story."

"Unfortunately, there is." Brooke went on to explain her encounter with Shannon that morning and all the threats she'd made. She pulled out everything that Shannon had threatened her with and handed it to Victoria.

Brooke stood and stared out the window while Victoria silently examined all the material. The pain in Brooke's lower back had increased as had the tingling in her hand, but Brooke knew she had to fight through it. There was only so much truth she was prepared to share at the moment. Fortunately, her pain was only an annoyance now and she planned to keep it that way. She closed her eyes and took a couple of slow cleansing breaths.

"My, my. The woman playing you in these photos is very flexible. And non-discriminative in her choice of sexual partners too."

Brooke turned and faced Victoria. "I swear that's not me."

"Of course, it's not. You could never do such things. Not to mention the fact that this woman doesn't have your birthmark."

"My birthmark..."

Victoria tossed the photos on the table and pointed at Brooke's left leg. "Unless you had it removed over the last few months, it was there the last time we all hung out at my pool not that long ago."

"My birthmark," Brooke repeated as she looked down at her leg. "I completely forgot about it."

Victoria pointed at the photos. "The woman in these pictures doesn't have your Florida birthmark and I'm sure the fact that you even have one isn't widely known."

"Which is why they couldn't copy it."

"It will be pretty easy to refute these photos. However, that police report is a different issue. What's the story?" Victoria asked, her lips pressed together.

Brooke pushed out a quick breath and returned to her seat. "Lisa and I spent a year going to school and working for Shannon. She convinced us it was an easy way to make good money. It was completely legit and she only hired college students."

"Completely legit until it wasn't," Victoria declared.

"It started off innocent enough. Just a few college girls offering companionship to a few older, wealthy men. There was never any sex involved. In fact, if Shannon even suspected that one of us was engaging in such activities, we'd be cut loose."

"When did that change?"

Brooke heard her phone ringing but ignored it. She knew she had to get through this conversation without distractions. "After Shannon's Prince Charming turned out to be a frog."

"What?"

"Shannon met and fell hard for a man she thought was The One. She thought she too had gotten lucky in love."

"Like your friend Lisa," Victoria concluded.

"Yes, only he lied to her. He was already married and had no intention of leaving his wife. What he did do was make Shannon his mistress and that changed everything."

"How?"

"She had a new vision for her business. Sex became an option for those who were willing. When she didn't get the response she was hoping for, she started hiring women who were more than willing to provide such services."

"Why didn't you leave then?"

"I tried to, only Shannon told me about some debt I owed."

Victoria shifted in her seat. "What debt?"

The tingling in Brooke's hand increased. "About a year after we started working for Shannon, things became more upscale. She made arrangements for us to have designer clothes and shoes and we started using a car service, or if the date was rich enough, we took a limo to meet them. At the time she said she'd worked out a deal with an upscale resale shop for our outfits and that the dates paid for the transportation. It was only when anyone tried to leave that we learned about all the money we owed her."

"Okay," Victoria replied, squeezing her hands together. It was one of the things that Victoria did when she was trying to stay calm.

"If I paid the debt with the money I had already made, I wouldn't have had enough for school. I agreed to stay and work it off for three more months during the summer."

"Where was Lisa at this time?"

"Lisa was married by then and traveling the world. She thought I'd already left the business too."

"Why didn't you call her for help?" Victoria asked, reaching for her ringing phone.

Brooke shrugged. "It was my mess to clean up, not hers."

"I see." Her mouth was set in a hard line.

"Do you need to get that?"

"No, continue." She put her phone down on the table.

"One night, I was sent to a party with a few other girls, none of whom I knew. There were lots of drugs, scantily clad women and a number of powerful men there—judges, politicians, and superstars. Before I could leave, the place was raided. The men were allowed to leave, but the women were arrested and charged with solicitation."

"Including Brooke Avery." Victoria's eyebrows snapped together.

Brooke nodded. She could feel the tears roll down her

face. "I pled no contest and was offered Deferred Adjudication, did thirty days community service and paid a fine. Once my case was dismissed, I changed my name to Brooke Smith, walked away from my past and never looked back. Until…until." Brooke couldn't get the words past the lump in her throat.

"Until you married my son."

"Yes," she whispered.

"Let me guess. Shannon came calling."

"Y-yes," she stuttered.

"So what? Shannon tried to extort money or blackmail you and instead of doing whatever she wanted, or going to your husband for help you decided to handle it yourself… again. And you asked Brice for a divorce and ran."

"Basically," Brooke replied.

"When will you children learn?"

Victoria rose from her seat and walked over to Brooke. She pulled her out of the chair and into her arms. Brooke broke down and cried like she'd never cried before. Victoria walked Brooke to the sofa and sat her down, filled two small crystal glasses with ice, then returned to the sofa and placed them on the table. Victoria pulled a pack of Kleenex out of her purse and handed it to Brooke, then took a silver flask out as well. Brooke wiped her eyes and nose as she watched Victoria fill the glasses with a gold liquid; whiskey, she guessed.

"You really need something stronger than water for times like these, my dear," she explained, handing Brooke a drink.

"Thanks." Brooke took several sips while Victoria tossed hers back so fast she figured the ice had had no time to do its job.

Victoria refilled her glass. "How much money do Shannon and her partner want from you?"

Brooke had left out a few details. "Actually, it's your

money they want, and a lot of it too." She got up, walked over to her desk and picked up the bank statement she'd printed out. Brooke handed it to Victoria and returned to her seat.

Victoria read the statement. "How did you find out about this account? This is an old personal bank account that only Elizabeth and I know about. It's not connected with the company." Her tone turned hard.

"Shannon gave me the information and I went searching for it. I still have all my old IRS contacts and connection with banks around the world, remember? It wasn't hard, especially since I had all the information I needed to access the account."

Before Victoria could respond there was a knock on the door. Brooke opened the door to a security guard holding a large box wrapped in a red bow. "Excuse me, Mrs. Kingsley, these came for you."

"Thank you," she replied as she accepted the box. Brooke closed the door and set the package on the conference table. She stared down at it as Lisa's warning about Shannon's tendency to send threatening gifts flashed through her mind. Brooke slowly removed the bow, lifted the top and smiled. A dozen long-stemmed roses lay on a bed of baby's breath. Brooke picked up a small white envelope and read the card: *I can't wait to see you tonight. Brice.*

"My son has excellent taste."

Brooke jumped. She hadn't heard Victoria approaching. "Yes, he does. About Brice..."

"You don't want him to know about any of this."

"Not yet. I want to be the one to tell him," she explained, hoping for her support.

"We need to figure out what we're dealing with and what we're going to do before we tell anybody anything," Victoria agreed, which overwhelmed Brooke with feelings of love and gratitude. They returned to their seats. "What did you mean, Shannon gave you the account information?"

"The card with the bank name and account number came with the pictures. This morning she claimed the money in that account belongs to her partner."

"What?"

"Yes, she said you stole it from him a long time ago, and they're just retrieving what's rightfully his, plus a little interest. Those were her words."

Victoria reached into her purse and pulled out a small tablet. She typed something into it and after a few seconds, she showed her a photo that now appeared on the screen. "Is this Shannon's partner?"

"I don't know. I've never met him. Who is he?"

"Evan Perez."

Brooke grasped. "That's the person Lisa found out was Shannon's partner."

"Lisa?"

"Yes, I asked her to see if she could find out who Shannon was working with and that's the name she was given. Who is he?"

"He's an old nemesis that's been trying to destroy my family for a very long time now. We just haven't been able to tie him to anything directly. Not even China's car accident."

"He was behind that too?"

"Yes, he was." Victoria stared down at the picture, her jaw tight.

"Why does he think you stole his money?"

"Because I did." Victoria put her tablet away and finished off her drink. "Let's just say it was a payment for a bad act."

"Some bad act."

"How do they expect you to move millions of dollars? It's not like you can carry it in your purse."

"Shannon gave me a list of bank accounts to send the money to."

Victoria's face lit up. "Really… Where is it?"

"I didn't take it. I told her I couldn't help her and I called you."

Victoria smiled, "No worries. She'll reach back out to you. There's no way Perez will walk away from this opportunity. Thanks to you, we just may be able to bring his reign of terror over our family to an end once and for all."

"Thanks to me?"

"Yes. When they contact you again, and they will, I want you to demand a meeting with her partner face-to-face. That way we can get his blackmail on tape."

"What if they say no?"

"Tell them if you're going to risk everything you need to be reassured that this will be the last time you hear from them and the only way you can be certain is to hear it from the man who's obviously pulling her strings."

"Okay. I'll just have to make it believable, especially after I said I'd never hurt my family."

Victoria squeezed Brooke's hand. "You're not hurting your family—you're helping us." Brooke smiled. "But you know we have to bring Brice and Alexander in on this. They both need to know what we're dealing with. Especially Alexander, considering what that man almost took from him," she explained, offering Brooke a sympathetic smile.

"I know you're right." She rose from her chair and walked over to the box of roses. "I just hate…"

"I understand, but trust me when I say, my son loves you and he won't care about your past. However, he will be pissed that you didn't tell him before now."

"I know." *And there's still so much more he doesn't know.*

"But he'll get over it too." Victoria gathered up her things. "I'm going to go see about getting us some professional help to trap this bastard and get him out of our life once and for all."

"Thank you, Victoria."

"Oh, sweetie, thank you for finally trusting me enough to help you." Brooke nodded, fighting off a new wave of tears. "Now, are you sure you've told me everything?"

"Well…"

Chapter 12

After Victoria finally left, it was a quarter until eight and Brooke felt like hundred-pound weights had been lifted from her shoulders. Brooke knew telling Victoria about her health issues was the right thing to do. Even though she had a difficult conversation ahead of her with Brice, she just had a feeling that everything was going to be fine. Even the pain in her back was subsiding.

Brooke put the photos and all the doctored material in the envelope, along with the police report and bank statements, and placed it all in her purse. Brooke smiled at the box of flowers. "I can't wait to see you too, Brice," she murmured.

The car ride back to the hotel seemed to take forever; she was so excited to see Brice. Brooke's mind flashed back to her last first date with him. Brice had rented out the Houston Museum of National Science so they could have a private tour; he'd heard she had a thing for mummies. Brooke smiled as she remembered how handsome

Brice had looked, standing outside the museum, waiting to escort her inside. She loved how ecstatic he had been about all the exhibits.

The best part about the date had been when Brice took her home and gave her a sexy kiss that overwhelmed all her senses. Brooke invited him in, knowing that if he'd asked to stay she'd have let him. However, Brice had other ideas. He told her what they were experiencing wasn't casual. Brice gave her one final kiss before whispering in her ear that they had lots of time. Brooke giggled at the thought. She couldn't wait to find out what Brice had in mind for their date tonight.

The car came to a stop and she exited. Brooke thanked the driver and hurried inside and upstairs. She was so focused on getting into her hotel suite that she didn't notice the hall was darker than normal or that her door's security lock had been dismantled. Brooke entered the dark room and closed the door behind her when suddenly she was hit hard from behind. She flew across the room, sending the contents of her bag and flowers everywhere, landing hard on the floor after bouncing off the coffee table and one of the chairs.

As Brooke cried out in pain, a large hand covered her mouth. The dominating figure, who she assumed was male, stood Brooke up and as she tried to fight back, the back of his hand came down hard across her face, cutting her lip. Brooke dropped to the floor. Her mouth filled with blood, her face stung and Brooke's eyes flooded with tears. She tried to speak, only the person picked her up by the throat, slammed Brooke's head against the wall and began choking her. Brooke clawed at the hands, gasping for air as her feet dangled above the floor. All Brooke wanted to do was survive so she could tell Brice how much she loved him and how sorry she was for everything.

"That's enough. We need her alive," the familiar voice instructed. Brooke recognized it instantly.

The hand loosened and Brooke slid to the floor. Her head was spinning. Coughing, trying to pull air into her lungs, Brooke brought her knees to her chest, lying on the floor curled up in a ball. "Please…stop" was all Brooke could manage between coughs.

"I think she's got the message," Shannon told the dark figure standing at her side. She knelt down and whispered, "You left the bank list at breakfast. I thought I'd bring it to you. It's on the bar. Do you understand what's expected of you now?"

"Yes," Brooke replied, barely above a whisper.

"Good. You have seventy-two hours to get it done. Don't make me have to come back."

Brooke lay there quietly as she watched Shannon and her male partner walk out the door. Riddled in pain and feeling like she was losing connection with her body, Brooke tried to get on her feet to no avail. As the room darkened, Brooke used her forearms to drag herself across the room to the desk. She pulled on the phone cord, bringing the wireless receiver crashing down on her. She listened for a dial tone and called the hotel operator.

"Good evening, Mrs. Kingsley. How many I assist you?"

"Help…me…" The darkness closed in on her.

Brice pulled his Bentley Continental GT V8 Convertible, one of the few toys he indulged himself with but rarely drove, into the parking lot of Brooke's hotel. He'd had every intention of stopping at the front door, only it was blocked by a fire truck and an ambulance. Brice parked as close as he could, walked the short distance to the entrance, hoping that whomever the ambulance was there for would be all right.

As he walked through the lobby toward the elevator,

Brice felt several eyes shift his way, which wasn't unusual lately, considering his family was always in the news for one reason or another. He refused to let whatever the latest Kingsley gossip was distract him from spending a wonderful evening with his wife. Brice couldn't wait to see the look on Brooke's face when she found out they were about to re-create their first date. However, tonight would end the way they had both wanted it to back then.

Brice smiled and nodded at onlookers as he waited for the elevator to arrive. He entered the car, hit the top button and rubbed his hands together like an evil villain in a cartoon. Brice couldn't wait to get his hands on Brooke.

When the elevator doors opened, Brice froze. The commotion in the hall caught him off guard. He stepped out of the car and saw two paramedics standing around talking. One said, "She won't go."

She. Brice's heart sped up and he nearly tripped on his own feet as he ran to Brooke's door. "Excuse me, sir," a large gentleman dressed in all black stated firmly, preventing Brice from entering the room.

"It's okay, let him in," a familiar voice instructed. It was Meeks Montgomery, COO of Blake and Montgomery, the security agency his family often used. Meeks was standing next to two women who were mirror images of one another and one large man that looked very angry, all dressed in black with guns on their hips. They looked like they were ready for war.

"Montgomery, what the hell's going on?" Brice frowned as he scanned the room. The place was a mess. Roses were scattered everywhere and furniture was toppled over. "Where's Brooke?"

"Brooke's in the bedroom with your mother and we're trying to figure out what happened."

Brice's frown deepened and his jaw clenched. "My

mother?" His voice rose slightly as he headed for the master bedroom's door.

"Wait." One of the two identical women stepped in his path, holding up her hands. "I'm Francine Blake Montgomery, and your wife has been through something horrific. She's going to need you to stay calm."

"Yeah, she doesn't need you going in there wilding out," her twin replied.

"Farrah, please, let me handle this."

The woman put her hands on her hips and said, "Handle it then."

"Sorry about that, Mr. Kingsley. That's my sister and business partner, Farrah Blake Gold, and that menacing-looking guy next to her is another partner, and Farrah's husband, Robert Gold."

Farrah offered up a half-smile and Robert nodded. Brice released a breath he didn't even know he had been holding. "We all know how you feel, trust me," Meeks stated, reaching for his wife's hand. "… But Francine is right. Brooke needs you to maintain your composure."

Brice fought to keep it together when all he wanted to do was burst through the door to get to Brooke. "What… happened?"

"She was beat up pretty bad, but she's refusing to go to the hospital," Meeks explained.

"Beat up? By who, and what do you mean she won't go to the hospital?" Brice's head was spinning as he was trying to make sense of what he was hearing.

"We're trying to figure that out now, but all Brooke wants is you…a calm you." Brice offered a quick nod. Francine opened the door to the master bedroom.

Brice crossed the threshold and stopped in his tracks. His eyes zeroed in on Brooke, who was sitting up in bed on top of the covers with her legs stretched out in front of her. She was still in her work clothes, her left hand was resting on her stomach and she was holding an ice pack against the lower half of the right side of her face.

Brooke lowered the compress and extended her right arm. "Brice…"

Brice was at Brooke's side in two strides. He sat on the bed and wrapped her in his arms. "Baby, are you okay?" he whispered.

Brooke nodded. "I am now."

Brice leaned back so he could examine her more closely. Brooke's lip was swollen and cut, her neck was red and bruised and she continued to clutch at her stomach. Brice was struggling to keep his anger under control. "Are you in much pain?"

Victoria's face twisted and her nostrils flared at his ridiculous question. "Of course, she's in pain, son."

Brice gently cupped Brooke's face and she laid her head against his palm. "Mother, can we have a little privacy, please?" he requested, holding Brooke's gaze.

"No. We don't have time for privacy." Victoria looked down at Brooke. "Do you want everyone in here or—"

Brice dropped his hand "Everyone? What's going on?" His eyes danced between his mother and Brooke.

Brooke reached for Brice's hand and squeezed it. "I promise, I'll tell you…everything soon just…be patient with me." She looked up at Victoria. "I'll come…to the… living room." She winced when she tried to move.

"Are you sure you should move? You need to see a doctor," Brice suggested, biting the instinct to carry her to the hospital himself.

"I'm sure. I have called…a doctor…already. Peter's on…his way. Things can remain private."

"Peter, your foster brother?" he asked, frowning.

"Yes."

"Stop making her talk," Victoria demanded.

Brice rubbed his face with both hands. He was losing

the desire to be patient. Brice wanted Brooke taken care of, and he wanted answers and he wanted them now. "Look—"

"Later, son. They're waiting." Victoria opened the door.

If Brice couldn't take Brooke to the doctor, he'd settle for the living room. He scooped Brooke up into his arms, carried her out of the bedroom and placed her on the couch where he took a seat next to her. The room had been cleaned and everything was back in its proper place. Meeks and his wife stood near the kitchenette and Farrah and her husband were standing near the balcony doors.

"What happened in here? How did this place get cleaned up so fast?" Brice asked no one in particular.

"We have a team that was waiting downstairs. They work very fast. Our crime scene technicians had come and gone just before you'd arrived," Francine said.

"I appreciate you all coming so quickly when I called. Where are we on finding the people who did this?" Victoria asked, standing with her arms folded across her chest.

Meeks stepped forward. "Shannon and her male companion are at her apartment." He turned his attention to Brooke. "Thanks to the information you provided, we think we may have identified the man that attacked you. Do you think you'd recognize the man who did this to you?"

"Wait, you know the bastard that did this and he's not in custody yet? And who is Shannon?"

Brooke could see the mixture of fear and confusion mar his handsome face. She reached for Brice's hand and intertwined their fingers. Here she was, in pain, and trying to comfort him. He loved her even more. "I'm…not sure. I never got—" she adjusted her position slightly "—a good look at his face."

"What about height or body type?" Francine asked, her voice calm. "Anything you can tell us will be helpful."

Brooke sighed, squeezed Brice's hand and closed her

eyes. Brice watched as Brooke recited in painstaking detail everything she'd gone through and even managed to
supply a brief description. Brice was experiencing a whirlwind of emotion, from anger to sadness to pride, and all
he could do was sit there and hope his silent presence was
giving her everything she needed.

Brooke opened her eyes. "I hope…that…that helps."

"Baby, you okay? Are you having trouble breathing?"
Brice asked, trying to control the panic he was feeling.

"I'm…just tired." She offered up a weak smile. "I'm…
closing…my eyes…for a while." Brooke lay down on her
left side with her arms wrapped around her stomach.

"Try to stay awake until the doctor can check you out,"
Brice insisted.

"What now?" Victoria asked.

"That depends on Brooke. She's in no shape to move
forward with the plan," Meeks advised.

"I agree," Victoria replied.

"Where's the doctor and what plan are you talking
about?" Brice stood and moved closer to where Meeks
and his mother stood. "Will someone tell me what the hell's
going on?" he demanded through gritted teeth.

"The people who broke in and attacked Brooke work
for Evan Perez," Victoria announced.

Brice felt like he'd just been hit hard in the gut by a
baseball bat. Memories of the pain they'd all experienced—
especially his brother Alexander—the last time Perez came
after their family had him riddled with fear. While fear was
an emotion he'd spent a lot of quality time with ever since
Brooke left him, this fear—fear for Brooke's safety—was
new. He looked over at Brooke's now-sleeping form and
vowed to himself to keep her safe no matter what.

"Evan Perez, are you sure?"

"Very," Victoria reassured.

"But why? He doesn't even know Brooke. Plus, as far

Dear Reader,

IT'S A FACT: if you answer 4 quick questions, we'll send you **4 FREE REWARDS!**

I'm not kidding you. As a leading publisher of women's fiction, we value your opinions... and your time. That's why we are prepared to **reward** you handsomely for completing our mini-survey. In fact, we have 4 Free Rewards for you, including 2 free books and 2 free gifts.

As you may have guessed, that's why our mini-survey is called **"4 for 4".** Answer 4 questions and get 4 Free Rewards. It's that simple!

Thank you for participating in our survey,

Pam Powers

To get your 4 FREE REWARDS:
Complete the survey below and return the insert today to receive 2 FREE BOOKS and 2 FREE GIFTS guaranteed!

"*4 for 4*" MINI-SURVEY

1 Is reading one of your favorite hobbies?
☐ YES ☐ NO

2 Do you prefer to read instead of watch TV?
☐ YES ☐ NO

3 Do you read newspapers and magazines?
☐ YES ☐ NO

4 Do you enjoy trying new book series with FREE BOOKS?
☐ YES ☐ NO

YES! I have completed the above Mini-Survey. Please send me my 4 FREE REWARDS (worth over $20 retail). I understand that I am under no obligation to buy anything, as explained on the back of this card.

168/368 XDL GMYK

FIRST NAME	LAST NAME

ADDRESS

APT. #	CITY

STATE/PROV.   ZIP/POSTAL CODE

READER SERVICE—Here's how it works:

as the world knows, we're getting divorced. Why would he think attacking my wife would hurt you in any way?" Brice questioned his mother, as he started pacing the room. "I mean, he's hell-bent on destroying our company because of something *you* did to him. Don't misunderstand me, you had every right to punish him for trying to hurt Aunt Elizabeth."

Victoria snarled. "Hurt? That bastard tried to sexually assault my sister. He put his hands on her. What I did to Evan Perez was nothing compared to what I could have done if Elizabeth hadn't begged me not to."

The room fell silent and Brice looked over at Brooke. He knew no matter how reasonable he tried to be when it came to avoiding violent confrontations, the apple didn't fall far from the tree when it came to protecting his family. He too wanted to harm the people who hurt Brooke.

"It makes no sense for him to come after Brooke."

"No, son, he doesn't know your wife, Brooke. But he does have a connection to someone with direct access to me. Brooke Avery."

Brice released an exasperated sigh. "Who's Brooke Avery and what does she have to do with any of this?"

"Brooke Kingsley and Brooke Avery happen to be the same person."

Chapter 13

Brice frowned, knowing he must have misunderstood his mother's words. "What did you say?"

"The woman—"

"I just need to close my eyes," Brooke mumbled a couple more times, capturing Brice's attention. He knew something was really wrong with her. He turned toward Brooke when there was a knock on the door and everyone froze.

"I'll get it," Meeks announced, moving toward the door. Brice watched as the others from his team positioned themselves in front of Brooke, his mother and even himself. But before he could inquire as to what they were doing, the door was open.

"I'm Dr. Peter Schultz," a man in running clothes and sneakers introduced himself. Standing next to him were two women dressed in scrubs, rolling bags on wheels behind them. "This is my nurse and mobile X-ray technician."

"Thank you for coming so quickly, Doctor. I see we must have interrupted your workout," Victoria guessed.

"Yes, but anything for… Brooke," he called out, making his way over to where she lay. He knelt down beside her. "Brooke… Brooke."

"What's wrong?" Brice's heart was racing so fast, pushing blood through his veins so loudly he could swear everyone could hear it.

"Brice," Brooke moaned with her eyes still closed.

"How long has she been this lethargic?" Peter asked, checking her pulse.

"Not long," Meeks advised.

"I need to move her to the bedroom," Peter announced. But before he could act, Brice stepped in and stopped them.

"Don't touch my wife. I'll take her." Brice didn't wait for a response. He gently picked up Brooke and carried her back to the bedroom. She felt light as a feather and looked weak. He carefully laid her on the bed, sitting on its edge next to her.

Brooke slowly opened her eyes. "Brice, you're still here."

"Of course, I am."

Brooke closed her eyes and Brice looked up at Peter. "What's wrong with her? Shouldn't we get her to the hospital?"

"That's not what she wants. If you'll leave us alone, we can do our job."

Brice was done being cordial. "I'm not—"

"Son," Victoria called from the doorway. "Come, let them work."

Brice didn't want to leave Brooke's side but he knew he needed to let the doctor do his job, not to mention he needed a few answers himself. Brice gave Brooke a soft kiss on the lips and whispered, "I love you." The words were out of his mouth before he could stop them.

"I love you too," Brooke replied with her eyes still closed.

Her words covered him like a welcome blanket on a cold winter's day; only Brice wasn't sure if Brooke meant it or even realized what she'd said but he chose to believe her words. Brice followed his mother out of the room, closing the door behind him.

"What did you mean, my Brooke and this Brooke Avery are the same person?" Brice asked, coming to stand next to his mother, who was making herself a drink at the bar.

Victoria picked up a bottle of vodka in a case adorned with Swarovski crystals and read the label. "Iordanov, very nice. Finally a hotel that knows how to treat their guests by providing a nice bottle of alcohol."

"Mother, that's a four-thousand-dollar bottle of vodka in the suite you *always* reserve. That bottle is to impress *you,* not most guests."

Victoria rolled her eyes skyward as she poured herself a drink. "If they really wanted to impress me they would've bought me a bottle of Russo-Baltique or Billionaire."

"Excuse me," the X-ray tech called as she entered the room.

"How is she?" Brice asked, feeling anxious for her response.

"Dr. Schultz is checking her now. I'm going to go develop the X-ray."

Brice sighed and ran his right hand through his hair. "Thank you, dear," Victoria said, encouraging the woman to leave.

"Can we get back to the question, please?" Brice's eyes scanned all the faces in the room before landing on his mother, who was sipping her drink.

Victoria pushed out a breath. "Son, there are a lot of things that you don't know about your wife's past—"

"Then tell me—"

Victoria raised her right hand, presenting Brice with her

palm. "You have every right to know—however, it's your wife's job to share it," she continued to explain.

Brice threw his hands up. "I don't understand any of this." His anger and frustration were about ready to boil over.

"What I *can* tell you, son, is that Brooke has history with Perez."

"History?" Suddenly Brice was not only fighting his anger but jealousy too. He knew Brooke hadn't been a virgin when they got together, but she told him she'd only had two boyfriends: one in high school and the other in college. Neither was Perez.

"Yes, and he's trying to use that history to blackmail Brooke. Convince her to steal half a billion dollars from us." Victoria poured Brice a shot and slid the glass in his direction.

"What?" Brice felt like his stomach dropped to his feet. "She wouldn't."

"You're right. She wouldn't." Victoria took another shot.

"Is that why this happened to her?" His nostrils flared. "Because she refused to help him?"

"Yes."

Brice picked up the glass and tossed back the drink. "How do we stop this bastard?"

Meeks stepped forward. "We have a two-part plan so that, if all goes well, Perez will be out of your life once and for all and behind bars where he belongs."

Brice ran his knuckles under his chin. "Don't keep me in suspense. What's the plan?"

Brooke... Brooke. She heard her name being called from what seemed like a long way away. Brooke slowly opened her eyes. A worried-looking Peter was sitting on the bed next to her. She felt as if her body had been shattered into a thousand pieces like a jigsaw puzzle and was slowly being put back together. But Brooke wasn't hurting as much as she had been. It soon felt like the pain was being held at bay by something pretty powerful and she found it easier to breathe.

"How do you feel?" Peter asked as he checked her vital signs.

Brooke swallowed hard. "Like I've been hit by a truck. Can I have some water, please?"

"How's the pain now? On a scale of one to ten."

"An eight, I guess. It's more like a dull whispering ache everywhere," she described, hoping she was being clear.

"Here you go, Mrs. Kingsley," a pretty dark-haired woman offered, handing Brooke a small glass.

Brooke accepted, noticing the tremors from earlier had gone. She drank the water and handed the glass back to the woman. "Thank you. Who are you?"

"She's my nurse, Sylvia," Peter introduced.

Brooke offered her a weak smile. "Where's Brice?"

"He's in the living room, standing in front of the door, I'm sure. We had to send him out so we could even examine you. He was like a security guard waiting to attack at even the slightest provocation. His instinct told him to take you to the hospital. I tried to assure him that I could handle things."

Brooke slowly tried to sit herself up in the bed and found it surprisingly easy to do, which was something she hadn't expected. "How *did* you treat me, exactly?"

"After we made sure nothing was broken, I figured your symptoms had to be related to your MS. The stress of the attack triggered an MS hug, so I gave you a shot of a pretty strong steroid and something to relax those affected muscles," Peter explained.

Brooke nodded. "I figured as much. I hit the coffee table and floor pretty hard, but I didn't think anything was broken. I guessed that there was only one reason the left side of my torso hurt and I couldn't breathe. I don't know why they call it an MS hug. To me, a hug is something pleasant. It shouldn't make you feel like a band is actually around your chest and ribs, squeezing the life out of you."

"That's because—"

"Stop!" She shook her head. "I don't need another clinical explanation."

"What are you going to tell your worried husband out there? They saw how out of it you were and you know the drill. You're going to need more infusions of those same meds to get through this episode."

"I'm going tell him the truth." Brooke swung her legs off the bed and sat on its edge.

"Finally."

"A version of it, anyway," she clarified.

Peter stood, folded his arms and glared down at Brooke. "What does that mean?"

Brooke could see the worry and frustration written all over his face. "Relax, Peter. I will tell him the truth, the whole truth and nothing but, only not right now. We have a threat to deal with that's more important."

Peter shook his head and sat back on the bed. "Look, I know I'm only your foster brother but you're pretty important to me *and* my family, so there's *nothing* more important to us than your health."

Brooke laid her head on Peter's shoulder. "You're all pretty special to me too and I know that's hard to believe sometimes with the way I keep everyone at arm's length, but I'm going to work hard at changing that. I promise. And I agree with you, which is why I'm so blessed to have you taking care of me. I just need a little more time before I tell Brice, and I really need your support on this."

Peter pushed out an audible breath. "What do you want me to tell him?"

"Just a watered-down version of the truth."

"Fine."

Brooke raised her head and kissed Peter on the cheek. "Now—" Brooke rose slowly "—whoa."

"You okay?" Peter stood and grabbed Brooke's hand.

"Yes, just a bit lightheaded. I forgot how this treatment feels."

"Where are you going?"

"First, to the restroom. I'd like to change clothes, then I'm going to go to talk to Brice."

"I'll go give him an update, then me and my team will go. I'll call you in the morning to check on you and figure out what time to come by for the second treatment."

Brooke raised her index finger as though she was about to excuse herself from church. "About the treatments…"

Peter frowned. "What about them?"

"I think I'd prefer the pills versus the IVs."

Peter held her gaze and slowly nodded his head. Brooke could almost see the lightbulb going off. "Yes, I guess it would be hard to explain IV fusions to your husband without telling him the truth, the whole truth and nothing but the truth."

"So you understand?"

"I understand what you're asking. It doesn't mean that I agree."

"But…"

"But I'll comply. I have enough doses with me of everything you'll need for the next couple of days. However, I'll have to send over more on Monday."

Brooke gave Peter a hug. "Thank you for everything."

"I'll call and check on you tomorrow."

"Nice to meet you," his nurse said to Brooke, following after Peter.

Brooke smiled and walked into the bathroom, feeling like she was walking through a fog that was slowly lifting. She knew she wasn't actually moving in slow motion but that's exactly how she felt. Brooke checked the mirror and frowned. She ran both hands across her face and cut lip before sliding them down to her neck. The bruises brought her anger to the surface. "Shannon, you're going to pay for this."

"So how is she?" Brice asked the moment Peter walked into the living room.

"She's better. Changing clothes right now. Nothing is broken, but she's pretty banged up on the inside. Her chest and ribs were bruised, which is why she was having difficulty breathing. I've given her something to relax those muscles and relieve the stress on her body."

"Thank you, Doctor. My family is in your debt," Victoria proclaimed.

"No need to thank me. Brooke's like a sister to me," he replied to Victoria. "I'll be checking on her over the weekend, but she has the meds she'll need for a few more treatments."

Brice offered his hand. "Thank you."

"Of course," Peter replied, shaking Brice's hand before leaving the room.

Brice turned to Meeks. "I need to make sure nothing like this ever happens again."

"It won't. I assure you," Meeks promised. "You know she's safe at work—your offices are like a fortress."

"And we've set up security on this floor, and she'll have protection with her everywhere she goes," Francine added.

Brice shook his head. "That's all well and good, but that's not enough. When Brooke leaves the office, *I* need to make sure she's completely safe."

"What do you have in mind, son?" Victoria questioned, brushing a piece of lint from her top.

"We're going to our place…"

"What about our place?" Brooke asked, walking into

the living room. She'd changed into a long white V-neck T-shirt and black leggings; her bruised face was free of makeup and her wet hair was pulled up into a high ponytail.

"Brooke, darling, you look so much better. How do you feel?" Victoria asked.

"Stronger, thank you." The corners of her mouth rose slightly.

Brice fixed his gaze on his wife. *After everything you've been through, you still manage to look stunning.* Brice took Brooke's hand and led her to the sofa, taking the seat next to her. "Can I get you anything?"

"Water, please."

"I'll get it," Francine volunteered.

Farrah's cell phone rang. "Excuse me." She stepped out into the balcony with Robert in tow.

"Here you go." Francine handed Brooke a glass and placed the half-empty water bottle on the table.

"Thank you." Brooke took several sips.

"If you're feeling up to it, we need to discuss where we go from here," Meeks encouraged.

"Yes, we do and I am," Brooke promised, placing the glass on the table.

Farrah and Robert walked in from the balcony. "We all set?" Meeks asked Robert.

"We will be," he answered with a quick nod.

"What are you talking about?" Brice snapped, his tone hard.

Brooke squeezed Brice's hand and smiled up at him. She looked at Meeks and said, "Please excuse Brice's rudeness. My husband's obviously upset."

Her husband. To Brice those words were like the sun breaking through the clouds. He brought her hand to his mouth and kissed it. "My apologies," he offered to the group.

"We understand. If you're still up for it Monday morning, you can make the transfer to the list of banks Perez wants, except you'll only be sending half the money to half the banks on the list."

"What? Why are we playing games with this maniac? Did I not make myself clear when I said that my wife will not get hurt again?" Brice barked, his nostrils flaring.

"No, you were very clear, and we all agree. However, we need to bring Perez out into the open," he explained to Brice before turning his attention back to Brooke. "After you send half the money, you'll demand an in-person meeting with Perez."

"Hell no! You're not putting my wife anywhere near that bastard."

"Son, it's the—"

"I'll do it!" Brooke declared before Victoria could even complete her statement. She looked at Brice and said, "It's not your decision."

Brice held her gaze. "Brooke—"

"No, the choice is mine. Besides, we're nearly divorced. You don't get a vote."

Chapter 14

Brice's face went blank and Brooke felt terrible. The words actually left a bad taste in her mouth. She reached for her water and finished it off. Brooke knew Brice was only looking out for her and she loved him even more for it, but she also knew he'd never allow her to take any risks unless she insisted upon it and this was the best way to make that happen.

Brooke hated appearing to be ungrateful but Meeks was right; this was the only way they could end the nightmare once and for all. She had to do everything possible to get Perez caught with his hand in the million-dollar cookie jar, so to speak.

The heartbreak she saw in Brice's eyes was more than she could handle. Brooke intertwined their hands and brought them to her heart. "I know you're worried and I appreciate it, but I have to do this…for us. I'll be fine." She turned her attention to Meeks and the rest of his team. "I will be safe, right?"

"Absolutely," Meeks promised. "We'll control the meeting location with Perez and you'll be perfectly safe."

"How can you be sure he won't have a weapon of some kind?" Brice's jaw tightened.

"He won't. The meeting will be at a restaurant inside Hobby airport," Francine explained. "He won't be able to get any type of weapon past the security."

"We'll have the restaurant packed with our people from the employees to the customers," Meeks informed her.

"So we're just going to give him thirty-five million dollars?" Brooke questioned with a deep frown, glancing at all the faces around the room and landing on Victoria. After all, it was her money; she should most certainly have a concern.

"Yes, but only for a short period of time," Meeks replied.

"What does that mean?" Brice asked.

"Yes, what do you mean by 'short period'?" Victoria echoed.

Meeks trained his eyes on Robert. "I'm going to let my esteemed colleague explain the details."

Robert offered a quick nod and said, "I developed a time-release snake algorithm and embedded it into each bank account." He gifted them with a proud smile.

"Allow me to interpret." Farrah gave Robert a smile. "My husband seems to forget that not everyone finds his IT-geek speech as sexy as I do."

"Farrah, please." Francine rolled her eyes skyward.

"What my brilliant husband is saying is that he set up a program that will track the money. Think of it like a bug. When they transfer the money out of those accounts, we'll know exactly where it's going."

"That's what I said," Robert mumbled.

"What if they try to pull out the cash?" Brooke couldn't believe she was even asking such a ridiculous question.

She just chalked it up to her head still being foggy from all the medicine.

"It's not like you can just pull out millions of dollars in cash, especially in a short period of time. That would certainly draw a great deal of attention," Robert explained.

"How can we be sure Perez is the one who's actually getting the money?" Brice questioned.

"We can't. Perez is too smart to have his name on any of these accounts, so I assume wherever he transfers the money to will be some type of shell company overseas."

"Which is why we need to get Perez's blackmail on tape," Francine reminded Brooke.

Brooke turned to Victoria. "That's a lot of money you could lose." Brooke's pain was reminding her of its presence.

Victoria gave a nonchalant wave. "That's my rainy day account."

Farrah's forehead creased. "Rainy day. What, you expecting a monsoon or something?"

Everyone laughed and Victoria shrugged. "You never know when you'll need a little emergency cash."

"A little," Farrah murmured. Francine gave her sister the evil eye.

"No worries. After ninety-six hours, my algorithm will self-destruct, reversing all transactions," Robert explained.

"I assume that means the money will revert back to my mother's account," Brice concluded.

"Correct," Robert confirmed.

"Seems easy enough," Brooke said.

"We should get moving. We have a lot to do still," Meeks suggested.

"My sister and I will help you pack. Come on, Farrah." Francine turned toward the bedroom.

"Packing? Where am I going?" Brooke asked, feeling confused.

"Do I look like a maid?" Farrah placed both hands on her hips. "I don't pack my *own* things."

"Excuse me." Brooke waved her right hand in the air. "Why am I packing?"

Brice turned and faced Brooke. He cupped her bruised cheek. "You're coming home with me, and before you say no, you're still my wife and it's my job to keep you safe. Please let me."

Brooke could see the fear that clouded Brice's handsome features and her heart raced as his words replayed in her head. She knew things were still up in the air between them but before she knew it, the truth was flying out of her mouth.

"There's no place I'd rather be." She leaned forward and kissed him gently on the lips. In spite of everything she'd been through, her desire for Brice was beginning to overwhelm her. "I'll go pack."

Meeks pulled out his phone. "I'll make sure everything's set up at the house."

Robert headed for the door. "I'm going to go clear a path to the back exit." Farrah followed Robert out the door.

"Back exit?" Brice inquired, helping Brooke to her feet.

"Yes, we will drive you both over in our vehicles. I'll have one of my men bring your car to the house."

"Is that really necessary?" Brooke asked, feeling weak but safe in Brice's arms.

"Yes. We want everything to seem normal in the event you're being watched. We'll place an agent in the room so to everyone that's watching it will appear that you're still staying here," Meeks elaborated.

"That way, if they try to come after you again here at the hotel, we'll catch them red-handed," Francine added.

"Do you think they'll try something like that again?" Victoria had concern written all over her face.

"No I don't, but we need to be prepared for anything,"

Meeks explained. "We'll even have someone acting as you leave from here going to the office Monday morning."

"We're just covering all our bases. I doubt they'll expect you to go, considering what they just put you through," Francine advised. "Your only job this weekend is to get better...stronger."

"No worries. I'll make sure of it," Brice promised, slipping his arm around Brooke's waist.

"Your place is already like a fortress so we'll just secure the streets," Meeks stated.

Victoria collected her things. "I'm going to go now. I need to fill the rest of the family in on these new developments."

"Victoria—" Brooke stepped out of Brice's hold and reached for Victoria's hand "—thank you. I can't tell you how much your support—"

"Child, please." Victoria kissed her on the cheek and turned to Brice. "Take care of her, son, or else."

"Yes, ma'am."

Victoria walked out of the room. Brooke stepped back into Brice's waiting arms. "What about the staff here?" Brice inquired.

"It's been taken care of. Everyone thinks Brooke had a slight accident in her room. Only the manager and security team will know what's really going on," Meeks informed Brice as he placed a call.

"Can we trust them?"

"We better. They're my team," Francine stated matter-of-factly. "This hotel has been our client since they changed owners and remodeled."

"I should go pack now," Brooke said.

"I'll help you." Francine took Brooke's hand and walked her back into the bedroom. Brooke was grateful for the assistance as her mind and body were still at odds.

* * *

Brice waited until Brooke crossed the threshold into the bedroom and Meeks finished his call before he asked, "You sure about this plan?"

"I'm sure this is the only way to catch Perez and stop him from hurting Brooke and your family ever again."

"Do you know what it is that Perez has over Brooke?"

Meeks sighed. "Yes, I do. But before you ask, I can't tell you. Brooke wants to be the one to share it with you. Just give her some space and a little time."

"I'm trying, but this is so damn frustrating. Everyone seems to know what's going on with my wife but me."

"I know it is, but you two love each other. That's pretty clear, so I'm sure you'll be able to work everything out."

"I hope so."

Meeks's phone rang. "Pardon me a second."

Brice gave him a quick nod and walked out onto the balcony. He was determined to be there for Brooke and protect her, no matter what it cost him. In order to achieve that goal, Brice knew he had to bring his emotions under control. Of all the Kingsley men, Brice was the most rational and thoughtful in making all his decisions. He was the least likely to be ruled by his feelings. Too bad his heart wasn't complying with his head.

He kept telling himself that, regardless of what might have happened in Brooke's past, he could deal with it. He loved her and nothing would change that. However, Brice was still determined to find out the truth from Brooke.

"Excuse me, Brice," Meeks called, stepping out onto the balcony. "We have a problem."

Brice turned and met Meeks's concerned gaze. "Another one?"

"After we determined there was no evidence to connect Perez to all the other crimes against your family, we placed one of our agents in his organization. My agent just informed me that Perez is making plans to leave the country…tonight, in about three hours."

"Tonight? Without the money?"

Meeks shrugged. "He doesn't have to be in town to collect his money, but we need him here if we're going to get him on tape."

"So what do we do?"

"We may have to move up our timeline," Meeks replied, scratching his chin with his index finger.

"To when?" Brice's brows snapped together.

"I'm not sure. My inside man is trying to get a more definitive answer on Perez's plans, but Brooke may have to make her phone call and threat to Shannon sooner than we initially thought."

"Dammit! I hate this."

"I understand, trust me, but it's the only way we can be sure to end this once and for all. We will keep her safe," Meeks promised before walking back into the living room.

Brice pulled out his phone and called his brother Morgan, the second eldest of Victoria's sons and the vice president of field operations.

"Brice, you good?" Morgan answered, sounding anxious.

"Not even a little bit. I assume Mother brought you up to speed on Perez."

"Yep, just hung up with her, as a matter of fact. That son of a bitch has to pay. How's Brooke doing?"

"She's fine, scared…even though I think she's trying to cover it up," Brice speculated.

"Why didn't she tell you someone was coming after her? You are her husband."

"That's a damn good question."

Morgan huffed. "Y'all think *I'm* an ass for not wanting to be involved with all the drama relationships bring."

Brice closed his eyes and shook his head. He was starting to regret making this phone call. "Relationships don't have to be full of drama."

"No, they don't have to be, but in my experience they usually are."

"Maybe it's the women you pick. Can you say—"

"All right. 'Thanks, pot,' says the kettle," Morgan replied, laughing.

"Fine. Look, I called for a reason."

"What's that?" Morgan rasped.

"Let me get A on the line first." Brice put Morgan on hold and called Alexander.

"Brice, Mother filled me in. How's Brooke?" Alexander answered.

"She's…dealing with things. Hold on while I patch Morgan in."

"Morgan?" Brice called out.

"Still here." Brice conferenced Morgan into the call. "All right, Morgan, you there?"

"Yep," he replied, sounding annoyed.

"Alexander?"

"Me too. What's going on, Brice?"

"You both know we're trying to set a trap for Perez. Get his blackmail on tape," Brice started, explaining.

"Yes, we know," Alexander replied.

"Well, we have a problem."

"What type of problem?" Morgan asked.

"Perez is scheduled to leave the country tonight unless we find a way to stop it."

"Me and a couple of the boys from the rig can pay him a visit. He can't leave the country if he's in the hospital," Morgan suggested.

"We can't get his confession, either, Morgan," Alexander scolded his brother.

"As much as I'd love nothing better, Morgan, Alexander's right. We have to find a legitimate reason to make him stay put," Brice said.

"Whatever. I still think he needs some pain put into his life for all the trouble he's caused our family," Morgan declared definitively.

"Morgan, physical violence against Perez, no matter how much I'd love to give him a taste of the same medicine he dished out to both my wife and China, that's not the answer," Brice said.

"So what do you have in mind, Brice?" Morgan asked.

"We give him the opportunity to get back something he's wanted for a long time."

"You can't be serious," Morgan said, his voice rising.

"Are you sure about this?" Alexander questioned; his concern was coming through the phone line loud and clear.

"Absolutely! Perez is a businessman. We need to give him a reason to stay put. We're going to give him the Carter."

Chapter 15

"Brice, you know how much that oil well brings in, not to mention it's a form of collateral for a few of our government projects," Morgan advised.

"I know. It's also the same well that Mom procured from Perez when she bankrupted him all those years ago. Do you seriously believe he won't stick around if he thinks he has a chance to get *that* well back? Especially if he thinks Mother's being forced to sell," Brice explained, feeling confident about his assessment.

"Mother will have to agree first," Alexander reminded Brice.

"If it will ensure Perez's presence so we can get him on tape for all his other crimes, including what he did to China and Brooke, I think she'll go for it."

"How do you propose to convince Perez, as well as the rest of the world, that Victoria Kingsley *needs* to sell anything, especially one of her most productive oil wells?" Morgan asked, his words draped in doubt.

"We'll leak the story that we're selling off a small division of the company that happens to include the Carter well to make room for another more lucrative acquisition. It's not like we haven't done that before. It will seem as if we're just getting rid of some dead weight for something more promising. When the story breaks, a diligent reporter will reach out to Perez for comment since the Carter was once his. They'll play up the throwaway aspect."

"And who is this diligent reporter?" Morgan asked.

"Morgan, I'm sure Kristen will think of someone. Lord know she knows enough reporters," Brice replied.

"What makes you think he'll buy it?" Morgan countered.

"Because he already wants money back he thinks Mother stole, he'll jump at the idea of getting everything," Brice reminded them both.

"Which includes the Carter," Alexander replied. Brice could hear the realization take hold in his brother's voice.

"Yes."

"As long as it's fake news, I'm fine with it." Morgan laughed.

"Yeah, well, our financial partners might not be too happy with the news," Alexander warned. Brice heard real concern in Alexander's voice and he knew if he couldn't get him on board, there was no way in hell his mother would agree.

"A, what if we get Mother to give our principals a call? Give them a head's up on what's going on," Brice offered.

"That could help."

"So we good?" Brice held his breath as he waited for his brothers' response.

"I'm good," Morgan quickly responded. "Although, I reserve the right to revisit laying hands on Perez if this doesn't work."

"Duly noted. A?"

"It's time for Perez to pay once and for all. If doing this will help ensure that happens and will keep our family safe, I'm in."

"We have to move quickly. A, can you talk to mother and get Kristen to get the story out?"

"Yep."

"Morgan, can you call KJ and Travis and bring them up to speed on what's going on? The press frenzy is about to start up again."

"Sure. Travis is going to be pissed."

"Yeah, well, what's new," Brice said.

"You'd swear that man was in witness protection the way he covets his privacy," Morgan said, laughing.

"Where will you be?" Alexander asked.

"With Brooke—we're moving her out of the hotel and back into our house," he explained.

Brice heard Morgan push out a deep breath. "Don't, Morgan," Alexander instructed, using his fatherly voice.

"No, A, let him say it. Morgan?"

"Do you think moving Brooke back into your house is a good idea?"

"Morgan, I've got to make sure she's safe."

"You can do that by letting the professionals protect her, change hotels, find a safe house—"

"That's enough, Morgan," Alexander interjected.

"I just don't want to see him hurt again," Morgan proclaimed.

"He's a grown man," Alexander reminded Morgan.

"I appreciate your concern, Morgan, and I honestly can't say how my closeness with Brooke will affect me or how things may develop with us, but it's a chance I'm willing to take. I love her," Brice admitted.

The phone went silent for several seconds before Morgan said, "I got your back, no matter what."

"Thanks, man."

"You take care of your wife—we got this," Alexander pledged.

"We have something like ninety minutes to make this happen," Brice responded.

"Ninety minutes? Mother can bankrupt a company in less than an hour." Morgan laughed.

"And that's what got us into this mess in the first place," Alexander said, sounding annoyed. "We'll keep you posted, Brice."

Brice disconnected the call and put his phone away. He headed back into the living room in time to see Brooke walk out of the bedroom, wearing sneakers and holding a bag in her hand. In spite of everything she'd been through, Brooke was still the most beautiful woman he'd ever seen and his body was responding in a way he wished it wouldn't in mixed company.

Brooke saw the corner of Brice's mouth rise and as their eyes met, her heart sped up. She gifted him with a lopsided grin. They were familiar gestures that they often shared only when they were alone and they would soon find themselves in bed. As she held his gaze, all the ways they'd made love flashed through her mind and her breasts felt heavy and her body ached for him. Brooke wanted him to finish what they'd started in his office.

"You ready?" Brice asked.

You have no idea how ready I am.

"Brooke…"

"Sorry, yes, I'm ready." Brooke was embarrassed by where her thoughts had taken her. The look on Brice's face made her think he could actually read her mind.

"The car is at the side door and Farrah's holding the elevator," Francine instructed.

Brice took Brooke's bag and placed her hand in his while Francine and Meeks grabbed Brooke's luggage. "Follow me and stay close," Meeks stated as they walked out of the room and into the hall.

Brooke thought this level of security was extreme but she wasn't going to complain, especially since Brice was by her side, no matter how brief that time period might be. Farrah stood in front of the open elevator. "Nice bags." Farrah stared down at Brooke's red Valextra Avietta luggage. "We bought a set for our sister not long ago."

Everyone entered the elevator and Brooke looked over at Francine before returning her attention to Farrah. "You two have another sister?" Brooke knew her confusion showed by the looks she was receiving.

"Yes, we're triplets. Born five minutes apart," Farrah explained, hitting the *down* button.

"Wow. Does she work with you too?"

"No, Felicia's a doctor. She's assistant director of the CDC. She and her husband live in Atlanta," Francine explained with a wide smile.

"Impressive," Brooke responded.

"I agree, but Felicia finds being the mother to her girls more impressive," Farrah added, laughing. "Don't get me wrong, I love my two boys but—"

"Farrah loves what she does just as much," Francine interjected.

"I am who I am," Farrah said proudly.

The elevator came to a halt. "Ready?" Meeks asked.

"Yes," Brice replied, and Brooke nodded.

Brooke remained quiet as they made their way through the lobby, down a small hall and out the side door to a waiting black limousine-style SUV. Her heart was suddenly heavy and she was fighting back tears. In spite of what the doctors might have said, Brooke was convinced that she wasn't destined to be happy long. Knowing she'd never know how it would feel to be a mother to Brice's children was breaking her heart all over again.

Brooke's curiosity was getting the best of her. "I read your bio, you're the only one with three children," she asked Francine.

"No, Felicia adopted a baby girl," Farrah answered for her sister.

"What?" Brice frowned.

Brooke was just as confused as Brice. "What he said."

"Long story short, Felicia and her husband Griffin adopted his biological child before they had children together, so they too have three children," Francine said.

"There's far more to it than that," Farrah said, laughing.

"That's a story for another day," Francine proclaimed.

Robert, who was riding shotgun, turned around and announced, "ETA is five minutes."

Brooke sighed. Her body was reminding her of everything it had been through that day. She laid her head on Brice's shoulder. "Are you okay, baby?"

No. "Yes, just tired and a little hungry."

After entering a gated community and driving several additional blocks, the vehicle came to a stop and they all exited. Brooke looked up at the gray brick house that had been the only place she'd stayed and ever truly lived in that she called home. She was overwhelmed with emotions as her mind flooded with the memory of the first time Brice brought her there. Right after they returned home from their honeymoon.

Brice carried Brooke across the threshold. "Welcome home, Mrs. Kingsley."

"Brice, what have you done?"

"I just wrote a check," he admitted, placing Brooke on her feet and offering a coy smile, trying to contain her excitement.

Brooke walked past the office, the mudroom and a half-bathroom into the open-concept house. The room was empty except for a small table set for two in the middle of the room, with a large pizza box and a bottle of wine on it.

"I suppose you have no idea how this food got here, either?" she inquired as she opened the box and took a whiff.

"That I can explain." Brice offered a mischievous smile. "I called Amy and had her set this up for me. I left a key under the mat and told her when we expected to arrive so the food would still be hot."

"Amy..." She quirked her left eyebrow.

"Yes, she's my intern."

"Your work intern," she countered, folding her arms across her chest. "I hope she left the key behind."

Brice pulled Brooke into his arms and kissed her passionately on the lips. "I love you, Mrs. Kingsley. You have nothing to worry about from Amy or anyone else. You know that, right?"

Brooke bit down on her lip, hating that she let her insecurity show in such a ridiculous way. "I know. Sorry, and I love you too, Mr. Kingsley. Now about the house."

"What about it? It's the only one we looked at that you liked."

"I know and I love it, but I thought we agreed that we'd buy the house together. Become co-owners."

"We did, and I love how independent and self-sufficient you are, but, Brooke, you're no longer alone. Just because you can do something by yourself doesn't mean you should. Not all the time, anyway. That's something my mother used to tell me, my brothers and cousins when she was trying to teach us to work together on things."

"I know, but—"

"Anyway, the house belongs to you. It's in your name. It's my wedding present to you."

Brooke's eyes widened. "What? I gave you a freaking pen because you collect them."

"I know and I love it."

"Besides, you gave me diamond earrings."

Brice shrugged. "The earrings were an accessory to your dress."

Brooke released an exasperated sigh. "What am I going to do with you?"

"I can think of a few things, but let's eat first," he replied, opening the bottle of wine.

"Fine, but I'm buying the artwork."

"Yeah, about that..."

"What about it?" Her eyes narrowed.

"I already set up a line of credit at the two galleries you like to shop at."

Brooke shook her head slowly. "How much, Brice?"

Brice poured the wine into the glasses and handed one to Brooke. "Twenty at each."

"Well, twenty thousand doesn't sound too bad." Brooke raised her glass, stopping before it made it to her mouth as she noticed the sheepish grin on Brice's face. "What?"

"Actually, it's twenty million."

"What?"

"Art is an investment," he defended himself.

"Rich people," she mumbled before drinking her wine. Brooke never imagined that she would find anyone to love her as much as she loved them or that he'd be so wealthy. She only prayed that she hadn't made a mistake.

"Is everything okay?" Meeks asked, snapping Brooke out of her reverie.

Brooke looked up at Brice and smiled. He winked at her, which told Brooke he'd been having similar thoughts. "Everything's fine," Brice replied as he led Brooke into the house.

Brooke walked into the living room and was hit by all the happy moments they'd shared and made. She was experiencing a rollercoaster of emotions as she held the hand of the man she adored. A familiar aroma had her stomach growling. "Chicken spaghetti?" She made her way over to the beautiful gray-and-white kitchen with its modern appliances that would make any chef drool.

Brice smiled, following after her. "You said you were hungry."

"Please tell me Amy didn't do this," Brooke asked, admiring the spread before her.

Brice laughed. "No, Mother had her cook make dinner for us, and her faithful assistant did some shopping too."

"We're going to take off now," Meeks announced, heading toward the door where Francine, Farrah and Robert stood.

Brooke was embarrassed that she'd forgotten her manners. "Wait, please join us for dinner. As you can see, there's plenty."

"No, thank you. We have a house full of children and nannies we should get back to," Meeks replied.

"Thank you for everything." Brice offered Meeks his hand.

"Just doing my job." Meeks returned the gesture.

"The team's in place at the airport," Robert informed them, putting his phone away. "But if Perez tries to leave—"

"About that." Brice held up his right index finger. "I put something in motion to ensure that Perez will stick around."

Meeks frowned. "Like what?"

"Brice, what did you do?" Brooke placed her hands on her hips.

"This could take a minute to explain," Brice stated.

Francine and Farrah pulled out their phones and called home. "Looks like we'll be having dinner together after all," Meeks said.

Brice spent the next hour going over his plans while

they all ate. "Not bad," Meeks complimented him. "Next time if you don't mind giving me a heads-up on what you're considering in the event we can provide some additional insight."

"I can do that," Brice agreed.

"Will Victoria go for it?" Brooke questioned.

"She already has. I got the text message on the way home."

"So, now we wait," Francine said.

"Yes, and there's no reason we can't wait at our own houses," Farrah said, getting to her feet.

After saying goodbye to their guests, Brice looked down at Brooke and asked, "Does it feel weird being here again?"

"Not at all." She shook her head.

"Not even compared to being in Paris?"

Brooke took a step forward, closing the gap between them. She placed her right hand over his heart. "Don't you know that *you* have always been my Paris?"

Brice's jaw clenched and she could see uncertainty in his eyes. Brooke held his gaze and said, "Take me to bed."

Chapter 16

Brice cupped Brooke's face with both hands and leaned down toward her as Brooke rose up on her tippy toes and wrapped her arms around his neck. Brice kissed Brooke gently and with reverence, struggling to remain in control of both his physical and emotional desires; only he knew Brooke wanted more. She pushed her body against his, swerving her hips, and something snapped inside of Brice. Their sweet, tender kiss turned passionate and full of need. Brice knew Brooke had been through a lot and no matter how difficult it was, he needed to slow things down.

Brice swept Brooke into his arms and carried her up the stairs, down the hall and through the double doors into their master bedroom. It was a room he hadn't slept in since Brooke left. *You can do this. You love her.* He lowered her onto the bed and removed her shoes. Brice ran his hands under her shirt, enjoying the feel of her smooth soft skin before pulling the shirt over her head, revealing a black bra, which he knew would be accompanied by sexy underwear.

When Brice ran his hands up her legs and along her inner thighs, Brooke moaned. Brice removed her leggings, revealing a pair of black lace panties. It had been so long since he'd seen Brooke laid out before him in such a way and his throbbing erection was reminding him of that fact. Her desire-filled eyes, the way she was whispering his name while he used his fingertips to stroke the tops of her breasts, was testing his ability to do the right thing.

Brice leaned down and kissed her gently on the lips as he lifted her slightly, pulling the covers out from under her. He placed the blanket on top of Brooke and said, "Not tonight, baby."

"What?" Brooke rose up on her elbows.

Brice sat next to Brooke on the bed. "Sweetheart, you know how much I want you—"

"And I want you too." Brooke sat up and kissed the corner of his mouth, running her tongue along his bottom lip.

"Baby, please, you need to rest. I saw you take another one of those magic pills Peter gave you."

"I'm fine," she claimed, lying back down slowly.

"No, you're not, and as much as I'd love to spend the night making love to you, I know you're not ready."

"I know what I want, Brice."

"My resolve *not* to take you now is weak, so if you can honestly tell me that you're one hundred percent better, then I'll be naked and inside of you before you can count to ten." Brooke released an audible breath. "That's what I thought. Now get some rest." Brice stood.

Brooke grabbed his hand. "Where are you going? Aren't you going to sleep in the bed with me?"

The corners of Brice's mouth rose. "I'm not sure that's a good idea."

"I won't attack you," Brooke teased.

"Not until I have an intense workout downstairs and a very cold shower, anyway." His eyes dropped to his crotch.

Brooke followed his line of sight and giggled. "Oh, okay."

"Anyway, I want to wait to see if we hear anything about Perez. Get some rest and I'll be up later."

"Promise?"

Brice leaned down and gave Brooke a quick kiss on the forehead, nose and lips. "Promise."

Brice walked out of the room, made his way downstairs to his man cave and changed into his workout gear. After putting on his boxing gloves, Brice spent the next thirty minutes beating and kicking his punching bag. He still couldn't believe his runaway bride was back home and in their bed. As he danced and moved, striking the bag, thinking about everything that Brooke had gone through, he began to burn off all his pent-up aggression. Just as Brice was about to step his worn-out body into a hot shower, his cell phone rang.

"So did it work?" he said as he answered the phone.

"It worked," Alexander replied.

"Yes." Brice pumped his fist. "Thanks, A."

"No, thank *you*. If you hadn't come up with the idea of using the Carter as bait to keep Perez here, we may not have had the chance to make him pay for all the damage he's caused. Now, let's just hope it works."

"Yeah, I just wish Brooke didn't have to be involved." Brice ran his right hand through his sweat-soaked hair.

"I get that, but she may be our only shot."

"You know what Perez has on Brooke, don't you?"

"Yes," Alexander confirmed.

"But you're not going to tell me, are you?"

"No, I'm not," Alexander replied.

"Listen, A—"

"No, you listen. Remember when I was going through

hell, when I was accused of stealing money from the company and intentionally putting the environment in danger with illegal disposal practices?"

"Of course…"

"I was going crazy," Alexander admitted. "And I can't count how many times you and the rest of the family tried to convince me that everything was going to be okay."

"What's your point?" Brice snapped.

"My point is it wasn't until *China* reassured me that everything would be fine and that she would be at my side no matter what that I finally started to believe it. No matter what I say, you won't be satisfied until you hear things directly from Brooke. She deserves a chance to explain everything herself."

Brice knew his brother was right. "Thanks, A."

"Anytime, bro…" Brice disconnected the call, jumped into the shower and allowed the body sprays of the multiple heads to do their job.

After fifteen minutes, Brice stepped out of the shower, dried off and wrapped the towel around his waist. He made his way back upstairs and into the master bedroom where he found a sleeping Brooke spread across the bed on her left side. She was out from under the covers, with her perfectly round behind calling out to him. Brice's eyes took their fill of the beautiful woman wearing sexy underwear, her hair sprawled across her pillow. His sex hardened instantly. His heart raced and he took short breaths as he stood there staring down at the only woman he'd ever loved.

Brice took a step forward, tripping over Brooke's travel bag, sending its contents and his towel to the floor. He froze and watched for movement. But Brooke just heaved a sigh and smiled in her sleep as she rolled onto her stomach, her head still facing away from him. Brice's eyes roamed her body and his right hand gripped his shaft as he started making long gentle strokes. He thought about how easy it would be to brush her hair to the side, kiss her neck and slide his tongue and lips across her shoulders and down her back just the way she liked it. Brice increased the pressure, knowing it would only take one kiss to wake Brooke and have her kissing him back. He could have Brooke's panties off and on the floor and be buried deep inside of her in seconds. Brice released a deep moan and before he even realized what was happening, he had found temporary relief of all his pent-up desire for Brooke in his hand.

"Dammit, man. What are you, fifteen?" he whispered, picking up his towel. Brice escaped to the master bathroom and jumped into another shower—a very cold one. After bringing his body back under control, he went to his closet and slipped on a pair of black silk pajama bottoms. When Brice returned to the bedroom, he picked up all the things that had fallen out of Brooke's bag. He noticed several bottles that weren't familiar to him. They certainly didn't contain the pills that had been given to her tonight, as they still sat on the nightstand next to the bed.

Brice knew he was crossing a line when he collected the bottles and started reading the labels. *What the hell is all this medicine for?* After returning everything to the bag and placing it back in its original spot on the floor, Brice made his way downstairs to his office where he fired up his computer. He began to research the medicines that Brooke had been prescribed. After reading pages of information on what each drug could possibly treat, reading blogs on those diseases and speculating what it all could mean, Brice walked over to his bar, poured himself a drink and tossed it back. He had an information overload and was angry that Brooke was obviously sick but hadn't told him anything about it. Brice went and sat on his sofa, stretched out his long legs and said aloud, "Looks like we have a great deal to discuss, sweetheart." Brice closed his eyes and laid his head back against the sofa.

Brooke stretched out her arms and sighed before opening her eyes. She was slightly disoriented and it took her a few seconds to recognize where she was and how she'd gotten there. "Brice," she murmured, raising the covers and looking down at herself. "Still dressed, I see. Brice, always the gentleman. I guess our making love was just a nice sexy dream."

Brooke sat up, slowly rotated her feet and hands, and was pleasantly surprised to find that the numbness was gone. However, her MS hug was still hanging on, although her breathing was back to normal and the tightening of her stomach muscles was loosening. Brooke got out of bed and her senses were assaulted by the smell of freshly roasted coffee and bacon, two of their favorite things.

After what seemed like the longest walk to the bathroom, Brooke's body wasn't ready for any mad dashes, she took a quick shower, hoping the hot water and body shower sprays would loosen up her muscles further. Brooke heard the bathroom door opening and she smiled. She had hoped Brice would be joining her.

"Good morning, handsome," she greeted, turning toward him. Her smile faded slightly, seeing that he was dressed in blue jeans and a white T-shirt; he was also in bare feet, holding a cup of what she assumed was coffee and a plate of bacon and scrambled eggs.

"Good morning," he replied, his tone flat and face expressionless.

"So much for that idea," she murmured.

"What was that?"

"Nothing. Why are you serving me breakfast in the shower?"

"When I brought up the tray, I thought I'd be serving you breakfast in bed," he explained.

"Oh, that was sweet of you, but I can eat downstairs with you," she replied, turning off the water.

"I ate already. I've been up awhile. I'll just put this back on the tray. You should eat while it's hot. Besides, you really shouldn't take all your medicine on an empty stomach," Brice advised.

All? Peter only gave me two prescriptions. Brooke wrapped her body in one of the big monogrammed towels that hung on the wall, her hair in a smaller version, and followed Brice out of the bathroom. "Is everything okay, Brice? Has something happened with Perez?"

"Everything is fine. Eat your breakfast, take your medicine and come downstairs when you're dressed." Brice kissed her on the cheek. "I'll bring you up to speed on everything. Take your time."

Brooke watched with a confused scowl as Brice walked out of the room, closing the door behind him. She wanted to go after him and demand that he explain what was going on with him, but her hungry body had other ideas. Her stomach growled, reminding her how much she needed to eat. Plus, Brice was right. She couldn't take her medicine on an empty stomach. Brooke walked over to the tray, looked down and smiled.

Brice had not only made her coffee, eggs and bacon, he'd also provided some fresh fruit, toast and orange juice as well. Brooke sat on the bed and finished off her breakfast faster than she'd expected. She reached into her travel bag and pulled out her daily maintenance medicine she took for her MS, adding them to the new meds that Peter had given her last night. Brooke still hadn't gotten used to the fact that she actually needed pills to help her stay healthy. She swallowed them all down with the freshly squeezed orange juice. Now that her stomach had been satisfied—at least one part of her body had been—and all her meds were on board, Brooke knew it was time to have the difficult conversation with Brice; she'd put it off long enough.

Brooke looked around the room to find where Brice might have placed her luggage. "Closet." She walked into the large walk-in with its mahogany wood and glass multi-level storage units to find that not only had her luggage been placed there but all the outfits she'd left behind several months ago were still there. The beautiful designer clothes and jewelry she'd left behind were still there and in their proper places. It was as if she had never left. Tears filled her eyes. Brice really hadn't given up on her. He'd actually held out hope that she'd come back to him.

"Brooke, you're such an idiot," she chastised her reflection bouncing off the mirrored wall. She took a deep breath and exhaled it slowly. "No more."

Brooke went to the area where she knew her casual dresses hung and pulled out a pink scoop-neck silk sundress. It was feminine and sexy and one of Brice's favorite outfits. She dried off and dropped the towels in the hamper before selecting a pink lace bra and thong set to accompany it—all of which she was hoping to be out of very soon. The thought made Brooke giggle. They deserved a second chance and she was determined to give them one.

Brooke put lotion on her body, lightly made up her face and blew her hair dry, leaving it down just the way Brice liked it. She pulled on her underwear and the dress and paired the outfit with a pink diamond necklace and earring set that Brice had given her. Brooke was excited and felt like she was getting ready for a date. She slipped her feet into a pair of white sandals and made her way downstairs.

Brooke stopped short when she heard Alexander's voice. Brice obviously had him on speaker. "You're right, man. She should've told you, but does it really make a difference?"

"Damn right, it does. It changes everything."

Brooke's stomach and heart dropped, and she suddenly couldn't breathe. Her excitement about their opportunity to be together and happy again evaporated as old demons took hold. She tiptoed back upstairs and ran to the bedroom. "So much for second chances."

Chapter 17

"Brice, how can you even be sure Brooke is sick? Did she tell you that herself?"

"No, she didn't and that's the problem. I'm not sure about anything. I'm only going off my own research. Brooke's not telling me a thing and neither are you, for that matter."

"We talked about this already," his brother reminded him.

"What if it was China? Wouldn't you want to know?"

"You know I would. Let me ask you something. If you knew she was sick before you got married, would you still have married her?" Alexander asked.

"Of course, I would have. I love her."

"And maybe you should ask yourself why she didn't trust you enough to tell you the truth."

Brice held his tongue as his brother's words took hold. "I think the way Brooke grew up makes her extra cautious when it comes to trusting anyone...even me. Earning the level of trust necessary for her to share such intimate details about herself takes time. Time I didn't give her."

"What do you mean?"

"I loved her and wanted to make her mine so much I didn't stop to consider that she might not be as ready as I was. We dated less than a year."

"But you worked together for a couple of years before that too. She loves you *and* she married you," Alexander reminded Brice.

"Yeah, but she also left me."

"So what are you going do about it?"

"Right now, I'm going to finish cleaning the kitchen. Thanks for talking me off the ledge, A."

"Anytime."

Brice heard China calling Alexander's name in the background. "You're being summoned. Talk later." He ended the call.

Standing alone in the middle of the closet, Brooke fought to bring her emotions and body under control. Surrounded by the trappings of her old life and Brice's actions of a concerned husband had had Brooke believing and dreaming that they could handle and get through anything together. The facts were different. "Stupid…stupid… stupid, Brooke," she scolded herself, swatting away tears "Stop it." *Pull it together, girl. You can get through this just like you've done your whole life…alone.*

Brooke took off the dress and hung it back where she'd found it along with the shoes and jewelry. She went over to her suitcase, pulled out a pair of black jeans and pulled them on. A short-sleeved green-and-black button-down shirt was the only accessory she needed. After removing the small amount of makeup she wore and pulling her hair back up in a messy ponytail, she picked up the breakfast tray and walked back downstairs in her bare feet with her head held high.

"There you are. I was about to come find you." Brice reached for the tray with one hand and Brooke's with the other. His touch sent shock waves through her body; everything about Brice plagued her.

Brice helped her down the last couple of steps. "How do you feel?" *Dizzy, sad and overwhelmed, thanks to you.* "I'm fine. Thanks for the breakfast. It was great," she complimented him.

"Did you take your medicine?"

"Sure did." *Swallowing those pills was easy compared to this one.* "Brice, we should talk."

"Yes, we should," he agreed, setting the tray down on the dining table before leading Brooke over to the living room sofa.

Brooke had forgotten how bright and beautiful the rooms were when the natural light came shining through all the windows. That was one of the main reasons they loved the house so much. Unfortunately, Brooke felt the light was now shining on the life she'd once had and was about to lose all over again.

Brooke forewent the sofa he offered and took a seat in one of the leather wingback chairs that had been placed across from it. She sat with her back straight and hands folded in her lap. Brooke knew she didn't look comfortable, which only matched how she felt, but keeping things professional was the only way she could get through the next few moments. As much as she could be, sitting barefoot in a house she adored, in front of the man she loved, who she knew was judging her based on past actions he could never understand.

"Brice, I really appreciate everything you did for me last night, but I think my staying here isn't the best idea." Brooke tried to keep her voice even and firm.

"Really, now?" Brice stared down at her with a curious look. He widened his stance and folded his arms across his chest.

"Yes. It just complicates things." She closed her eyes and shook her head, hoping the tears that stung her eyes wouldn't fall.

"How so?"

Brooke released a quick breath, opened her eyes and looked up at Brice. "Please sit down."

"If that will make you more comfortable." Brice dropped his arms and sat on the sofa, resting his elbows on his knees. "How's this? Better?"

Brooke could hear the annoyance in Brice's voice that he was clearly trying but failing to hide. "Much, thank you."

"Now, why don't you explain to me why is it that my wife, who's in danger and risking her life to protect my family and our business from a vengeful maniac, shouldn't let me…her husband…protect her in their home surrounded by a top-notch security team?"

Brooke slumped back into her chair. "When you put it like that…"

Brice dropped his head and released a sigh of frustration, one she'd heard many times before while working together. He stood, walked over to Brooke and knelt down in front of her. His right hand cupped her face. "Talk to me."

A flush crept up Brooke's face and her whole body came to life at his touch. She couldn't think clearly when he put his hands on her. Brooke's nipples were hard and she needed to cross her legs to release the pressure building. She was fighting hard not to fling herself into Brice's arms. *Focus, Brooke.*

"There are a lot of things about my past…about myself, that I know I should've shared a long time ago."

"And why didn't you?" He dropped his hand.

Brooke shrugged. "Scared, I guess. I'm so used to handling things on my own."

"But you're not on your own anymore." Brice stood and started pacing the room. "You're my wife and you've kept things from me…important things. Things that alter the direction of our marriage."

"I am sorry." Brooke wiped away her tears.

Brice stopped midstride and said, "I am too. I'm sorry you didn't let me help you."

Brooke shook her head. "There's nothing you could've done."

Brice's cell phone rang. "I have to answer this. I'm expecting an update on Perez."

"No problem." Brooke needed the distraction. She rose from the chair, picked up the tray of dirty dishes and entered the kitchen to find her cell phone also dancing across the countertop. "There you are."

Brooke picked up her phone and read the missed text messages she'd received from several individuals regarding the Carter rumors Brice had set up. Her phone vibrated again; only this time she was receiving a call from a caller with a blocked number and she knew who it had to be.

"What do you want, Shannon?"

"Good morning, sunshine."

"What do you want?" Brooke repeated.

"Just checking to see if you're doing okay this morning."

"I'm fine, no thanks to you and your henchmen."

Shannon laughed. "Good, because I need a small favor."

"Favor?" Her voice rose slightly. Brooke looked over her shoulders to make sure she hadn't caught Brice's attention.

"Yes. I need you to meet me—"

"Hell no. I'm not coming anywhere near you ever again."

"You don't have a choice. However, to prove what a

good sport I am, I'll let you pick the location. Make it as public as you like, only come alone," Shannon demanded.

"Why do you need to meet me in person, anyway?"

"There's been a change of plans," Shannon announced.

"What kind of change?" Brooke pressed.

"You'll find out when I see you. So, where will we be meeting in two hours?"

Brooke thought about the one public place that would be full of people with an area where they can meet and open enough that she could see Shannon approaching from any point. "Hermann Park...the zoo. Meet me at the big concession stand after the main entrance."

"Outside, really? You know how much I hate the heat."

"You should probably get used to it since you'll be roasting in hell one day."

"But until then, I'll see you at noon." Shannon disconnected the call.

Looking down at her phone she mumbled, "How do you pull this off, Brooke?"

"Sorry about that," Brice said, reentering the kitchen. "With all the recent media attention online about our little announcement, we're now getting pushback from one of our equity partners about the Carter."

"I thought Victoria called all the partners and informed them of what was really going on with the Carter."

"She did, but this particular partner wants to try and take advantage of the situation," he explained.

"That can't be going over well with Victoria." Brooke reached into the cabinet and pulled out a glass. She opened the refrigerator, retrieved the orange juice and filled her cup. "Want some?"

"No, I'm good. I need to go into the office for a bit. I know we need to finish our conversation—"

"Don't worry about it." She waved her hand.

"No, Brooke. We need to talk things through."

"We will. But for now, you need to go take care of business. Lori's coming over, anyway." *Note to self: call Lori.*

Brice's forehead creased. "She is?"

"Yes. I'd go stir crazy sitting around doing nothing, and I need her help on a project." Brooke took a sip from her glass.

Brice's frown deepened. "Shouldn't you be resting?" He knew one of the meds Brooke was taking was to combat fatigue.

"I will," Brooke raised her right hand. "Promise."

Brice closed the space between them and Brooke slowly lowered her hand. He stared down at Brooke and smiled. "You're the most beautiful woman I've ever seen." In spite of all the lovely things Brooke had to wear, Brice like it best when she was relaxed and dressed casually.

Brooke captured her bottom lip between her teeth and shifted her weight from one leg to the other. "Thank you."

Brice ran the back of his right hand down the side of Brooke's face. "I love how soft your skin feels against my own." Brice slid his fingers across her lips before capturing her chin with his thumb and index finger. He raised Brooke's head as he lowered his toward her. Brice kissed Brooke gently on the lips. He leaned back and stared into her eyes. "Everything's going to be fine. I promise. Together, we can get through anything."

"Can we?" she whispered, wrapping her arms around his neck.

"Yes." Brice picked Brooke up and sat her on the edge of the island. He stood between her legs, buried his hands in her hair and devoured Brooke's mouth.

Brice lost himself in her taste. The slide and pull of their tongues ignited his hunger for Brooke and he had to touch her. Brice unbuttoned her blouse, slid his hands inside and under her bra, massaging her breast and sending his blood racing south to his groin. Brooke moaned in Brice's mouth. Unable to deny their lungs oxygen any longer, Brice ended their kiss but moved his mouth to her breast. Brooke's head fell back, offering him what they both needed. Brice sucked and pulled until he heard Brooke whimper his name.

Brice fought hard to break through the hurricane of desire they were both engulfed in, to bring himself back under control. He was only moments away from taking Brooke right then and there in their beautiful kitchen. Brice leaned his forehead against hers, breathing hard. "I have to go, but I'll be back soon." Brice helped Brooke down and gave her another not so quick kiss before walking through the living room to the stairs, taking them two at a time to put on his running shoes and heading out the door. Brice was annoyed he had to leave Brooke with so much unresolved and for a brief moment he worried that she might not be there when he returned.

Brooke's shoulders dropped and she released an audible sigh. She adjusted her bra and buttoned her shirt. "I should have told Brice about Shannon's call. Maybe it's time you start trusting your husband a little more," she chastised herself. "But first, *I* have to deal with Shannon." Brooke picked up her cell phone and dialed Lori.

"Brooke, what's up?" She could hear surprise and curiosity in Lori's voice, especially since they rarely spoke on the weekends since Lori's engagement.

"Sorry to bother you on this beautiful Saturday morning, but I was hoping I could get you to do me a small favor. That is, if you're not too busy right now." Brooke held her breath, hoping Lori would give her the response she desperately needed.

"I'm not busy—what do you need?"

"How would you like to go with me to the zoo?" Brooke asked, sniggering, imagining the look on her friend's face.

"What?"

"I need to meet someone there in about an hour and a half, but I don't want to drive or take a car service."

"Why are you meeting someone at the zoo, of all places?"

"It's a long story, and I promise I'll fill you in on everything," Brooke assured her.

"I'm not going to like this, am I?" Lori guessed.

"Probably not."

"Does this have anything to do with all those sketchy phone calls you pushed off as nothing?"

"Will you come?"

Lori groaned. "Of course, I'm coming. I can be at the hotel in thirty minutes."

"Thanks, I'll tell you everything when you get here and yes, it does have to do with those phone calls. But I'm not at the hotel, and I need you to wear that long maxi sundress I bought you."

"A sundress? Why? Wait, did you say you're not at the hotel?"

"Yes, I did and I'll explain when you get here."

"Where's here?" Lori asked.

"Home."

"Home…as in your house with Brice?"

"That's the only home I've ever had, so yes."

"Wow, a lot has happened in twenty-four hours."

"You have no idea. See you soon." Brooke disconnected the call, made her way upstairs and to her closet. She selected a multicolored maxi sundress and leather sandals. After Brooke changed clothes and selected two pairs of sunglasses and two tan hats, she looked in the mirror and said, "Time to get creative."

Chapter 18

Brice walked into the windowless executive conference room of the Kingsley building to find his brothers Alexander and Morgan sitting across from each other in red leather wingback chairs at the six-seat oval mahogany table.

"What the hell happened?" Brice asked, taking a seat next to Alexander.

"It seems that Bob Rosenstein wants to renegotiate our deal because the Carter well is no longer viable collateral for our investment."

"That's ridiculous. Rosenstein knows our deal is solid and the Carter isn't going anywhere, right? Mother did speak to him." Brice's eyebrows stood at attention.

"I most certainly did talk to him and he knows our securities in his investment house are solid," Victoria announced, walking into the conference room in a black pantsuit that reflected her mood.

All three Kingsley men stood and greeted their mother

with a hug and kiss on the cheek. "Bob is just trying to squeeze out a few more perks."

"What kind of perks? These are multi-billion dollar business deals, not a damn ice-cream parlor where he can get free scoops whenever he wants it," Morgan replied, his tone hard.

"Can't we just stall him until we wrap this thing up with Perez on Monday?" Brice suggested.

"Hell no, we're not playing games with that fool," Alexander stated.

"We have to make Perez think that the Carter is up for grabs. Otherwise, he'll take off," Brice reminded everyone.

"And we will, son. I have something else in mind for Bob Rosenstein."

"We can't afford to make another enemy, Mother," Brice declared as Brooke's face popped into his mind.

Victoria took a seat at the head of the table. "He knows why this has to be done. That I'm trying to protect my family and he's trying to take advantage of the situation. He's made himself an enemy, son."

"What do you have in mind, Mother?" Brice's curiosity was piqued; as long as it didn't involve or hurt Brooke, he was open to anything.

"The Patterson Group," she announced.

Brice face twisted. "What about them?"

"Yeah, what about them? You know they hold the paper on two of Perez's most recent deals," Alexander reminded his mother.

"True, but they'd prefer to work with us, which means…" she prompted.

"We won't need to do business with Rosenstein anymore," Brice concluded.

"Are you sure the Patterson Group has the same resources as Rosenstein? They've been securing our overseas interests for years." Morgan leaned back in his chair and scratched his head.

"Absolutely, who do you think Rosenstein's overseas resources are?" Victoria announced, raising her left eyebrow.

Brice sat forward in his chair. "You mean Rosenstein has been fronting all this time."

Victoria nodded. "Yes, Patterson has been underwriting all of Rosenstein's overseas businesses for the past few years. I guess, technically, they've always been working for us."

"I bet they're tired of giving the credit away for their work," Morgan said.

"Not to mention the commission," Brice added.

"How can we be sure Rosenstein won't blow the whistle and ruin the sting on Perez when he finds out what we're doing?"

"They won't. First, we have a nondisclosure agreement, so if they say anything they'll get sued and lose millions. Second, they won't know about the change until after the sting is done," Victoria assured them confidently.

"So, what, you're going to agree with his terms, then renege? We don't play those games, Mother," Alexander insisted.

Victoria pointed a diamond clad finger at Alexander and said, "No, son, you don't play those games and nor should you. You're not the CEO of my company. It's not your decision."

Alexander shook his head. "We have a reputation—"

"Yes, one based off business ethics I put in place a lifetime ago. Now for the record, I'm only going to agree to think about it. By the time they receive their ninety-day termination letter, Perez will be locked away in some jail cell." Victoria picked up her buzzing phone and read an incoming message.

Brice released an audible sigh. "And Brooke will finally be safe."

"Excuse me." Victoria walked out of the room.

"While we're all together, let's hammer out a quick outline for this new deal," Alexander suggested.

"Let's make it quick. I want to get back to Brooke," Brice said, smiling, thinking about the nice moments they'd spent together before he left.

"I *cannot* believe you talked me into doing this," Lori stated, adjusting her hat and sunglasses in the mirror of the zoo's bathroom. "What's the deal with the stupid outfits, anyway?"

"What? You said you liked the dress when I bought it for you last year."

"I do. I love multicolored print maxi dresses. They're light and very sexy."

Brooke ran her hand down the front of the near replica she wore. "Then what's the problem?"

Lori turned away from the mirror and faced Brooke. "The problem is we're dressed like twins, wearing big hats and sunglasses, playing spy games in the zoo and chasing some crazy person."

"We're not chasing anyone. You said you wanted to help me stop Shannon and her partner," Brooke reminded her nervous friend.

"Yes, but I meant help with finding him or even creating a paper trail to nail his ass. Not chase bad guys in the middle of the zoo."

"If you don't want to do this, I understand. You can wait for me back at the car."

Lori frowned and tilted her head slightly. "I don't want either one of us to do this. After last night, how could you even think about getting anywhere near that woman and not tell Brice what's going on?"

"I don't have a choice. Shannon said to come alone."

Lori threw her hands up and shook her head. "And you just do it."

Brooke laughed so hard at the look of exasperation on her friend's face she snorted. "It'll be fine."

"The sister inside your biracial behind should've told you to stay your butt at the house until Brice got back so you two could figure out what to do next together."

"What's your excuse for helping me?" Brooke said, as she and Lori acknowledged the two young women that entered the restroom.

"I'm your friend and assistant. That's what I do. But the minute I see something I don't like, I'm calling 911 and I'm hauling ass out of there. Got it."

Brooke giggled. "Got it."

"Are you sure you're feeling up to this?"

"I'm fine."

"What's the plan again?" Lori nervously looked over her shoulder.

"What are you doing?"

"I'm making sure we're not overheard," she whispered.

Brooke pressed her lips together to keep the smile she wanted to release at bay. "When we leave here, we head to the fountain. You go out first and a few minutes later, I'll follow you. Once we get there, you go left and I go right. You hang out at the entrance area and act like you're checking your phone or something but keep your hat and glasses on."

"What will you be doing?"

"I'll be hanging out at the concession stand, waiting for Shannon to meet me. There's always a ton of people around. She won't try anything in such a public place."

"You hope so, anyway."

Brooke could hear the concern in her friend's voice and while she'd never admit it, she was a little scared. However,

her fear for what Brice might do if he was in the same vi-
cinity as Shannon scared her more. While she knew he'd
never lay a hand on Shannon physically, he would have her
arrested on the spot, putting their whole plan in jeopardy.

"And what am I a diversion for again?"

Brooke checked her watch. "The security team trail-
ing me. With all the sundress-and-hat-wearing women
out here, add the fact that we're basically the same height
and size, and we should easily blend in. Hopefully, they'll
follow you to the front, buying me some time before they
start looking for me."

"This plan seems…"

"Simple."

Lori placed her left hand on her hip. "Reckless."

Brooke reached for Lori's hand and gave it a quick
squeeze. "It's going to be fine. I'm sure of it."

"If you say so."

"Ready?" Brooke plastered on a fake smile, feeling
thankful that Lori could not hear how loud her heart was
beating.

"Nope, not at all. Let's go." Lori walked out of the
restroom.

After several seconds, Brooke peeked out the door and
as expected, the two security guards that had followed her
from home were now on Lori's trail; their black outfits
were hard to miss. Brooke took a deep breath and exhaled
slowly. She pulled out the phone, opened the recording app
and texted Shannon.

After receiving her reply, Brooke exited the bathroom, checking for more men in black as she made her
way through the zoo over to the concession area. Brooke
smiled as she thought about all the times she and Brice had
spent in both the park and the zoo. She only hoped they
would get a chance to do it again. Their attraction for one

another was undeniable. It was just her past and present issues she wasn't sure they could get through.

Brooke spotted an empty table near several families and sat down. She scanned the crowd for Shannon, spotting her leaving the line at the concession stand holding two bottles of water. The big man standing behind her sent a wave of panic throughout Brooke's body and she suddenly couldn't breathe. Brooke just knew it was the same man who had hurt her the night before. She reached for her purse and cell phone and was about to run, only her fear-riddled body made it impossible for her to move. When she saw the man head in the opposite direction, her lungs started working again. Brooke watched until he disappeared into the crowd.

"Hello. Hello." Shannon snapped her fingers in front of Brooke's face.

Brooke swatted away her hand. "Stop it."

"Just making sure you're still with me." Shannon sat down and handed one of the bottles of water to Brooke. "You should have some. It's getting really hot out here. I'm glad I wore this romper."

"No, thank you. You agreed to come alone. What's that animal doing here?"

"I agreed to *meet* you alone. Besides, where else should animals be than in the zoo?" Shannon laughed, lifting her sunglasses off her face and placing them on the table.

"What do you want now?"

"Not so fast. How do you feel? Things got a little rough last night." Shannon took a drink from her bottle.

"What do you want?" Brooke repeated, her tone firm. She refused to give Shannon the satisfaction of knowing how much pain she had been in and was starting to feel even now.

"What I want is for you to remove your damn sunglasses and loosen the hell up," she ordered through gritted teeth.

Brooke dropped her shoulders, removed her sunglasses and hat, placing them both on the table. She ran her hand through her hair and smiled. "Better?"

"Much. Now take the water and act like you're glad to see your old friend. That way, the security team I'm sure the Kingsleys have on you won't think anything is wrong and interrupt us before our business is complete."

Brooke complied, cracked the seal of the water bottle and took a drink. She only hoped Shannon couldn't see the shake in her hand that she was trying to hide. "What makes you think I have a security team?"

Shannon rolled her eyes. "You may be getting divorced but you're still a Kingsley that's worth millions. You'll always have some sort of security, especially after last night. Speaking of which—" she took another drink from her bottle "—what did you tell everyone about what happened? My contact at the hotel said you were taken to the hospital but returned sometime later."

Wow, Meeks's plan had really worked. "I told everyone I walked in on a robbery and that I didn't remember anything. They checked me out and sent me home."

"Good girl."

"How could you be sure I wouldn't tell everyone the truth? I could've had you both arrested."

"You could have and yet you didn't. You have too much to lose…to protect." Shannon pulled out a business card from her back pocket and handed it to Brooke.

Brooke read the card. "What is this?"

"That, my dear, is the routing number to my personal overseas account where you'll reroute five of the seventy million dollars you'll be sending Monday morning."

"You mean five million of the blackmail money you're making me steal from the Kingsleys," Brooke clarified.

"I'm not making you do one thing. You have choices."

"Some choice, pay you or you'll destroy my life…my family's life…with the pack of lies."

Shannon smirked. "What's a few more lies? Your whole life has been one big lie, Brooke Avery Smith Kingsley."

Shannon's words stung but Brooke knew part of what she was saying was true. She had lied to Brice when she hadn't told him about her past or her illness—but that stopped today.

Chapter 19

Brice checked his watch and phone. He'd texted Brooke that he was running late but hadn't received a response yet. "So we good?" he asked, feeling anxious to get back to the house.

Alexander slid several documents across the table for Brice to review. "You tell us. You're the numbers man."

"I'm good with everything, except the additional points on the back end. I think it's too much."

"Me too, but we don't have a choice," Alexander said, cracking his knuckles.

"That's the way things are done in oil-rich countries with governments basically for sale," Morgan added.

Brice sat back in his chair and checked his phone again. "I guess." Alexander and Morgan looked at each other before turning their attention back to Brice. "Go ahead. Say whatever it is you need to say."

"I know you're worried about Brooke, but she can take care of herself. She has for years. We need your head in the game," Morgan replied, leaning forward and resting his forearms against the table.

That's the problem. She wants to do everything herself. "My head is in the game. Like you said—" Brice folded his arms "—it's how things are done and the price of doing business in other parts of the world."

Victoria walked back into the conference room and her expression hardened. "What now?" Alexander asked.

She returned to her seat, tossed her phone on the table and said, "What is it with the women you boys pick?"

Morgan was single and had no intention of changing that fact, either, so he reached in his pocket and pulled out his phone and started checking his messages. "That question is definitely for you two."

"What's going on, Mother?" Alexander questioned.

Victoria tilted her head and glared at Brice. "Do you know where your wife is at the moment?"

"Yeah, she's home with her friend Lori." His face went blank. "Isn't she?"

"Not unless you've recently moved into the zoo."

"What?"

"Apparently, she's enjoying this lovely day playing detective or something. She's meeting with Shannon, one of her blackmailers, at this very moment."

Brice jumped up, sending his chair flying backward. "She's where? Doing what?"

"You heard me right. She's at the zoo, meeting with Evan Perez's partner in crime."

"How do you know this?" Alexander asked.

"I just got a text from security," she replied.

"Why didn't anyone call me?" Brice picked up his phone to make sure he had indeed missed a call.

"Because I told them I'd handle it, and it's my name on the check," she reminded Brice.

"Excuse me." Brice started for the door.

"And where do you think you're going, son?"

"That would seem pretty obvious, Mother." Morgan placed his phone on the table. "He's running to the rescue."

Brice turned and glared at his brother. "What is it with you? What do you have against Brooke?"

Morgan stood and crossed his arms. "Oh, I don't know, maybe just the fact that she lied to you, took off and now she's playing damsel-in-distress."

"That's where you're wrong, big brother. Brooke is no damsel-in-distress, and how about you not push your issues off on my wife?"

Morgan raised both hands in surrender. "My bad."

"Enough." Victoria slammed her palm on the table. "Brice, you're not going anywhere. Brooke is covered, and she didn't ask for your help."

"That's the problem," he murmured.

"Do you know what's going on, Mother?" Alexander asked.

"I have no idea, but I'm certainly going to find out, only later." She rose from her chair and walked over to Brice. "We have to let this thing with Shannon play out, son. Trust that Brooke knows what she's doing."

Brian ran his hands through his hair. "Fine, I'll wait."

"Looks like we're done here. I'm going to hit the road." Morgan picked up his phone and walked over to where Brice was now standing. "Look, man, I didn't mean to—"

"Don't worry about it." He held out his fist. "I know where you were coming from and we're good." Both men bumped fists before Morgan walked out the door.

"Mother, maybe you should leave this one up to Brice. I'm sure he'll fill us in as soon as he knows something." Alexander turned toward Brice. "Right?"

"Of course," Brice promised.

"Fine, talk to Brooke. Find out what's going on with this Shannon-person but make sure Brooke understands that I expect her to follow the plan. Blake and Montgomery are in charge of this investigation."

"Yes, ma'am."

Victoria collected her things and left the office. Brice gripped the back of the closest chair and released a string of profanity. "Feel better?"

"Not really, but maybe after a few rounds with my punching bag."

"Then go home, get in a good workout while you wait for Brooke to return. Then talk to her." Alexander walked over to his brother and patted him on the shoulder. "About everything."

"I will. Thanks, A."

"Fine, I'll do it." Brooke agreed to Shannon's request, reluctantly smiling at all the kids that passed by.

"Good. Now, I don't know about you, but I'm going to go check out a few of the animals."

"I hear there's an excellent shark exhibit. You should feel right at home."

Shannon rose from her seat and smiled down at Brooke. "Aren't you cute? You just make sure all the transfers happen first thing Monday morning. Call me when it's done," she yelled over her shoulder as she walked away.

Brooke watched Shannon until she faded into the crowd. She pulled out her phone, turned off the recording app and texted Lori her location. Brooke saw that she'd missed several messages and calls from Brice but figured she'd be better off dealing with him in person, so she texted that she was fine and would be home soon. As she sat and waited for her friend to join her, Brooke watched as the people walked by and one young couple wearing *Mr.* and *Mrs.* T-shirts caught her attention. She thought back to when she and Brice had eloped and exchanged wedding vows at the Falls Wedding Chapel in Niagara Falls. The location was special to them because it was near the hotel where they'd spent their first night together.

"Brice, this place is gorgeous," Brooke complimented, staring up into his eyes. The stunning secluded outdoor garden Brice had selected for the ceremony was just a short walk from the falls.

"It's just an understudy to my beautiful star." Brice leaned down and kissed her gently on the lips.

Brooke knew her face had turned scarlet, but she didn't care. She'd never been so happy. "Thank you."

"That dress is perfect," Brice said.

Brooke looked down at the strapless lace floor-length dress with a sweetheart neckline and smiled. "I still can't believe you found someone who could make all this happen, including finding me this perfect dress, in less than forty-eight hours."

"The perks of being a Kingsley," he admitted.

"A Kingsley. I'm about to marry a Kingsley." Brooke bit down on her bottom lip. Her heart started racing and she suddenly couldn't breathe. Yes, she loved Brice, but the idea of becoming a Kingsley scared the hell out of her. Growing up in the foster care system taught her not to trust the good stuff. It never lasts.

Brice intertwined their hands. "You're about to marry me... Brice. A man who loves you more than anything or anyone else in this world. You're mine and I'm yours." He brought their hands to his mouth and kissed the back of hers. "Nothing or no one will ever come between us. I promise."

"I love you too," Brooke replied. Brice pulled his right hand free and wiped away her tears.

Brice's face lit up. "Are you ready to make it official?"

Brooke pushed out a quick breath. "I'm ready."

* * *

"Are you all right?" Lori questioned, breaking Brooke's connection to the past.

"Umm…yes, I'm fine."

"Then why are you crying? Did Shannon say something bad and threaten you?"

Brooke wiped away tears she hadn't realized she had shed. "Nothing I haven't heard before."

Lori took a seat next to Brooke. "Then what's going on?"

"I just remembered something Brice told me the day we got married. Something I'd forgotten. Something I'll never forget again," she promised herself.

"That's good, I guess. What did that crazy lady want?"

"More money," Brooke admitted.

"Did your plan work? Did you get her confession on tape?"

"Yes, but the only person she incriminated was herself and maybe her henchman."

"Well, that's something," Lori concluded.

"It's not enough to end all this," she said.

"What now?"

Brooke heaved a sigh. "Now I go home and have that long overdue conversation with my husband."

"What are you going to tell him?"

"The truth. I'm going to do whatever I can to try and save my marriage."

Lori smiled. "It's about time. Before we go, can we stop and get a corn dog?"

Brooke laughed. "Sure. I could go for some cotton candy myself." She reached for her hat and sunglasses, putting them back on as they made their way to the concession stand.

As they weaved their way through the crowd, Lori stated, "You know, this has been a very productive day."

"How do you figure that?"

"You finally realized you want to stay married," Lori concluded.

The corners of Brooke's mouth turned up. "Yes, I have. I just hope Brice still feels the same way."

Brice read Brooke's text message again and shook his head. He still couldn't believe that she had gone to meet Shannon on her own after everything she'd been through. He didn't know if he should be proud of her or furious. Right now, he was leaning more toward furious. He spent the next forty minutes taking his frustrations out on his punching bag. With each punch he threw, the less frustrated he became and the more determined to convince his wife that no matter what they had to deal with they could handle it together.

"Enough…" Brice reached for a towel and wiped away the sweat falling from his face. After taking off his boxing gloves, Brice walked upstairs to his kitchen, removed a large bottle of Gatorade from the refrigerator and drank it down, standing in front of the open door. He placed the empty plastic bottle in the recycling bin, made his way up the next level to the master bedroom and tossed his phone onto the bed.

Brice walked into the bathroom and had just removed his clothes when his cell phone rang. He walked naked into the bedroom and picked it up.

"Yes, A?"

"Any word yet?"

"Only that she's okay and will be home soon. That was about an hour ago."

"Well, the good news is she's fine," Alexander offered.

"Yes, she is," Brice said, his voice even.

"According to Meeks, Perez is staying put, so at least we know that part of the plan is still on track."

"There is that," Brice said sarcastically.

"Let me know if you find out anything."

"Will do." Brice disconnected the call and placed the phone on his nightstand. He walked back into the bathroom, turned on the shower and stepped under the multi-headed spray. Brice needed to douse the raging fires of desire and frustration he was feeling toward his wife.

Lori pulled into Brooke's driveway. "Home sweet home."

Brooke looked out of the passenger side window at the beautiful house that Brice had given her and said, "Yes, it is. And to think I nearly let it slip through my fingers."

"So, you're still going to tell Brice the truth about everything and fight for your marriage?"

"Yes, of course."

"Just checking. It's not like you haven't changed your mind before." She gave Brooke the side-eye. Brooke stuck out her tongue. "Oh, that's mature."

Brooke opened the door and stepped out of the car. "Thanks for your help today."

"Anytime."

Brooke walked into the house, expecting to find Brice waiting in the living room for her; only he wasn't anywhere around. She walked upstairs and the closer she got to the bedroom the clearer it became as to where Brice was.

She walked into the bathroom and found Brice standing in the shower with both arms extended and his palms pressed flat against the wall. While water rained down on him, Brooke's eyes roamed his wet naked body and her nipples instantly hardened. She leaned against the door frame and admired his thick thighs and his firm round butt and decided they could talk later. She quickly undressed, dropping her clothes to the floor, and walked into the bathroom.

Chapter 20

Brooke opened the glass shower door and stepped inside. She ran her hands across Brice's muscled back and snickered when she heard him gasp. "Care if I join you?" Not waiting for a response, Brooke peppered kisses across Brice's broad shoulders.

"Brooke…"

"Yes, baby," she replied in a hushed tone. Brooke reached around his leg, gripped his thick erection and started making slow deliberate strokes.

"I… I think…damn," he whispered. Brooke watched as he flexed his arm muscles. It was as if he was using every bit of his strength to hold up a falling wall. It was his way of maintaining control of himself. The heat from the shower was nothing compared to the desire raging through Brooke's body.

Brooke released Brice, stooped under his arms and stood in front of him. "I know we need to talk and we will. I promise I'll tell you everything, but right now I need to make love to my husband."

Brice gazed down at Brooke. His eyes were dark and filled with a passion that she knew matched her own. He dropped his arms and closed the small space between them. "How do you feel?" His voice was every bit as husky as hers.

Brooke could see that Brice was fighting for control, something she needed him to lose. She placed her palms on his chest and slowly slid them up until they were around his neck and her naked body was pressed against his.

"I'm fine, but I'll be a whole lot better once you're inside of me." Brooke swiveled her hips against his sex and got the response she wanted.

Brice captured Brooke's mouth in a kiss that sent fireworks throughout her body. He lifted Brooke off her feet and she wrapped her legs around his waist. "Yes, baby…"

Brice held Brooke against the wall with one arm and guided his shaft to her entrance with his right, teasing her and allowing himself only a taste. "Damn, Brooke. It's been too long."

"Pl-please." Brooke came down on Brice as he pushed himself deep inside of her. "Yes… Brice… Yes," she screamed. The pace they set was manic and it visibly tested Brice's ability to keep them both upright. They held nothing back, allowing them to reach unbridled satisfaction together. After all the additional positions they tried in the bathroom, Brice and Brooke were weak and completely spent. They wrapped themselves in large towels and made their way to the bed where they collapsed in each other's arms.

"Baby, you sure you're okay? That last position couldn't have been too comfortable. That tub seemed bigger."

Brooke laughed. "I'm fine. It's not like we haven't done that before, you know."

Brice closed his arms around Brooke and kissed her on the forehead. "I love you."

Brooke leaned back and looked into his eyes and replied, "I love you too. More than I ever thought possible." Then she yawned. "Sorry."

"Don't be. Get some sleep."

Brice heard his phone buzzing as he forced his heavy lids to open. The darkness of the room had him slightly disoriented. He looked down and saw the most beautiful set of eyes filled with yearning staring back at him. "Brooke…"

"Were you expecting someone else?" She rolled on top of him kissing and licking his smooth chest. It didn't matter that they'd woken and made love once already. Brice could see the overwhelming need she had for him and he loved it. It was like it had been when they first got married.

"Never."

"Good." Brooke rose up on her knees and stared down at him. She wrapped her right hand around his bobbing sex and placed his tip slightly inside of her. "I'll never share you."

"You won't have to," he promised.

Brooke lowered herself onto him, taking him inside. She crossed her arms over her head, closed her eyes and slowly rotated her hips, losing herself in the moment. Brice gripped Brooke's hips with both hands and followed her lead, matching her stroke for stroke. He watched in awe as she used her hands to pull and squeeze her breasts. Brooke was doing all the things she knew he liked.

Brice fought his instinct to rise up and take them in his mouth but Brooke clearly wanted control and he had every intention of letting her have it. Brooke seemed to be trying to erase the last few months they'd been apart and it was working. The damage she'd caused to his heart was slowly mending. When Brooke's walls began to contract,

Brice's thin line of control snapped. He sprang forward like a panther after his prey, curved his arms around Brooke's body and flipped her onto her back. Brooke's laughter sent chills throughout his body.

"My turn," he whispered before passionately kissing Brooke on the lips and setting the pace that had them reaching complete satisfaction simultaneously.

"Wow…" Brice rolled off of Brooke and onto his back.

"Wow…is…right," Brooke managed between breaths. "You're…incredible."

Brice turned his head toward her. "No, baby, we're incredible…together." Brooke smiled and nodded in agreement.

"I…" Brooke's eyes filled with tears.

Brice turned onto his side and held up his head with his left hand while he wiped away Brooke's tears with his right. She often cried after they made love so intensely. She'd told him once that it was because their love overwhelmed her with joy. Now, he was only hoping that that was the reason for these tears.

"Sweetheart, are you okay?"

"Yes."

Brice smiled. "Happy tears?"

"Mostly."

Brice's heart skipped several beats. "Mostly?"

Brooke moved onto her side and faced him. "Yes, it's just we have so much to deal with and I don't want to lose this connection. It's fragile, and I know that's my fault, but I want a chance to fix it."

Brice exhaled a slow sigh of relief as he took his right hand, removed a wayward strand of hair that had fallen in Brooke's eyes and placed it behind her ear. He needed the small distraction so he could pull himself together. He stared into Brooke's teary eyes and said, "You're right. We do have a lot to discuss and several things to deal with and we will. Only we're doing it together. The love that I have for you—"

"That we have for each other," she corrected.

Brooke's declaration made Brice feel like he'd just stepped out of the darkness and into the sunshine. He plastered a wide smile on his face. "Yes, that we have for each other will see us through anything." Brooke released a fresh batch of tears, nodded and pulled Brice to her, kissing him as if she had something to prove. Brice's body instantly responded and so did Brooke's. She pushed him onto his back and captured his erection with her left hand. Brice knew where her next kiss would be but he heard his phone buzzing again. Brice reluctantly said, "Baby, I have to get that."

Brooke flopped back onto her back. "Fine."

Brice reached for the phone and checked the time. "Brooke, it's almost nine."

"No wonder I'm so hungry."

Brice looked over at Brooke and cocked his head. "Oh, *that's* why you're so hungry," he said sarcastically. Brooke covered her face and giggled. It was a sound he'd missed and would never get tired of hearing.

"I've missed several calls from Alexander, Morgan and my mother."

Brooke quickly sat up, bringing the sheet to her chest. "Victoria? How many times did she call?"

"Twice. Why is it that my mother can elicit such responses from you but I can't?" he teased.

"Because she's scary."

"True."

Brooke dropped the sheet, exposing her breasts and rock-hard nipples. "Only you can do this to me."

Brice knew they were acting like sex-crazed teenagers, but he didn't care. He figured his family had waited this long; a few more minutes couldn't hurt.

* * *

Brooke smelled Brice's fresh woodsy cologne before she felt his warm lips graze hers. She opened her eyes to find a fully dressed Brice sitting on the bed next to her, holding a large coffee mug. The bright sun rays were being held at bay by the room's blinds, but she knew it was early the next morning.

"Good morning, baby." Brice offered her the cup.

"Good morning." Brooke sat up and wrapped herself in the sheet. Her body ached but not from her MS and that made her smile. She accepted the cup and took a sip. "French vanilla, my favorite."

"I know. Go take a quick shower and come downstairs." Brice stood.

"Why? And why are you dressed?" Brooke loved him in blue jeans and a white T-shirt but right now, she wanted him naked and back in bed with her. "It's Sunday. I thought we could spend the day in bed." She gifted him with a smile before taking another drink from her cup.

Brice smiled down at her. "That would be wonderful, but we have company downstairs."

"What…who?"

"My mother and Aunt Elizabeth."

"Oh, my goodness." Brooke handed Brice her cup, got out of the bed and sprinted to the bathroom.

After brushing her teeth, Brooke took a fast shower and then clipped her hair high up on her head. She went to her closet and pulled out a set of underwear, a pair of blue jeans and a blue blouse. Brooke dressed quickly and slipped her feet into a pair of slippers. She gave herself one last look in the full-length mirror. "This will have to do." Brooke made her way downstairs, feeling as if she'd been summoned to the principal's office.

Brooke walked into the living room where Victoria sat in one of the wingback chairs; dressed in black Chanel head-to-toe, she was looking very annoyed. Brice walked in from the kitchen, holding a tray of plated food followed by his aunt Elizabeth, who was wearing an all-white version of Victoria's outfit.

"Good morning. Wait…" Victoria checked her diamond encrusted watch. "Yep, it's still morning…barely."

"Good morning, Victoria," Brooke responded.

Brice placed the tray on the coffee table next to a pitcher of orange juice and several glasses. Elizabeth walked around Brice. "Good morning, Brooke. Forgive the intrusion, my dear." She pulled her into a warm embrace.

"It's not a problem. You're always welcome in our home." Brooke looked over at Brice, who was standing next to his mother, smiling.

"Aren't you sweet? We brought a Spanish sausage quiche. I've already sliced it up. It's our form of an apology for stopping by unannounced."

"No, *you* brought them a quiche and we have nothing to apologize for. Had my calls been answered or returned last night this visit wouldn't have been necessary." Victoria scowled at Brice.

"Victoria, please." Elizabeth sat in the chair that was twin to Victoria's. "They needed a little quality time together."

Brooke could feel her face, not to mention other parts of her body, start to warm as her eyes collided with Brice's. "Brooke…Brice, sit down," Elizabeth instructed, gesturing toward the sofa. Brice reached for Brooke's hand and led her to where they could sit facing both women. Brice intertwined their hands.

"You're both right. We did need time together, but I should have answered your calls, Mother. I apologize," Brice admitted, his eyes moving from his mother to his aunt.

Elizabeth gave a nonchalant wave and smiled. "It's fine."

Victoria's forehead puckered as she stared at her sister. Brooke bit her bottom lip to keep her laughter from escaping. "Now, let's have some of this wonderful quiche before it gets cold." Elizabeth picked up one of the plates.

Victoria rolled her eyes skyward. "Let's not. We have business we need to discuss."

Elizabeth's lips drew back in a snarl and she gave her sister the evil eye. The room fell silent. Brooke felt as if this whole mess was her fault and she needed to do something about it. "We can do both." Brooke picked up two plates and handed one to Brice. She took her fork, sliced into the quiche and tasted it. "Wow. This is delicious. Brice, take a bite." Brooke took several more.

Brice did as she asked and nodded. "Good."

A wide smile spread across Elizabeth's face as she sat back in her chair and ate her own food. "Now, can someone please tell me what happened yesterday?" Victoria asked no one in particular but leveled her eyes on Brooke.

"Yes, Victoria." Brooke wiped her mouth with a napkin and placed it on her plate. "I got a call from Shannon yesterday, requesting that I come meet her." Brooke explained everything that occurred during the meeting in great detail to a very attentive audience. She could feel three sets of eyes boring into her face.

"So, now she wants you to steal from the money she wants you to steal," Victoria recapped with a curious look on her face.

"Yes."

"I assume you agreed?" Victoria asked.

"I did," she replied.

"Why did you go meet her alone?" Brice questioned, turning his body toward Brooke.

"Those were her terms," she explained.

"It didn't mean you had to meet them," Brice countered, his tone hard.

"She most certainly did," Victoria defended.

"I knew I had my security, so I wasn't really alone."

"The same security you ditched, you mean," Brice clarified.

"It was necessary," she murmured.

"Why, because you were afraid I'd find out the truth about you?"

Chapter 21

Brooke's heart started racing and beating so hard, pushing blood through her veins, that she was afraid they might actually burst. Brice's jaw tightened and his expression hardened. The room was as quiet as a library. Brooke wanted to break their connection and ask Victoria if she'd told him everything after promising she wouldn't, but it really didn't matter how he found out.

Brooke dropped her shoulders, raised her chin and stared back at Brice. "I was going to tell you today." Brooke's eyes fell to her hands, which were now intertwined together and resting in her lap as she fought to keep her tears in their ducts.

"Were you now?"

Brooke could hear the doubt in his voice. "Yes." Her worst fears were coming to life. What if he hadn't meant it when he said they could get through anything together? *Stop it. Remember what Victoria said. He's going to be pissed, but he loves you so he'll get over it.* "Just a little later. I wanted a few more hours of bliss before we had to deal with everything."

"Victoria, let's give these two some privacy," Elizabeth stated as she rose from her seat.

"Yes, of course."

Brice stood and walked his mother and aunt to the door. Brooke collected the dirty dishes, returned them to the kitchen and start putting them in the dishwasher. A dull pain was creeping up her torso; it was the beginning of an MS episode that she didn't need. Brooke was about to head upstairs to get her medicine when she noticed it was on the counter next to the coffee pot. She selected the bottle she needed.

"What—"

"I figured you'd need to take them," Brice explained, walking into the kitchen.

"That was very thoughtful of you," she replied, doling out the required dose. She turned to find that Brice had removed a water bottle from the refrigerator and was handing it to her. "Thank you."

"Sure." Brice took a seat at the island; his arms were folded across his chest. The muscles in his jaw twitched, but his eyes had softened. Brooke didn't know if he'd brought his anger under control himself or if his mother or aunt said something to him. Either way, she was grateful.

Brooke twisted the top off the bottle, popped two pills in her mouth and chased them with the water. She took the stool across from him. "Is that all you need to take?"

Brooke nodded. "For now."

"So…" he prompted.

"I apologize. I should've told you everything about myself before we got married."

Brice nodded slowly. "I deserve the truth. I should've known about anything and everything that could have an impact on our future before we got married."

"I just… I didn't… I just didn't…" she stuttered, having trouble getting the words past her lips.

"You just didn't what…trust me?" he concluded.

Brooke swiped away a lone tear that had escaped. *Just be honest.* "No, I didn't. I wasn't sure you could handle the truth about my world, my life. Not given where you came from. How you grew up."

"What does that—"

Brooke raised her palms to stop his protest. "I know you understand loss, probably better than I do, because of your father. But what you don't get is the concept of being totally and completely alone. Having no one to depend on but yourself. When bad things happen to you or if you have to make difficult choices, you just handle them. It's like you go on autopilot. I'm sorry I didn't trust you."

"And you had every right not to," Brice replied.

Brooke recoiled. "What did you say?"

Sadness clouded his features. Brice stood, came around the other side of the island, took the seat next to Brooke and turned his body toward her. "When we first met, I thought you were the smartest and most beautiful woman I'd ever met. You were also the most guarded," he said.

"True. To the guarded part, I mean," she clarified.

"See, you still have no idea just how stunning you are." He ran the back of his index finger down the side of her face before dropping his hand. "Once we started getting to know each other, I fell for you hard and fast. I was determined to sweep you off your feet."

Brooke cupped his face with both hands. "You did, and I fell hard for you too. I've never been so happy in my entire life," she admitted.

Brice gripped her wrist and gently removed her hands from his face before intertwining their fingers.

Brooke's words and touch sent a warm feeling throughout his body, igniting his desires, and all he wanted to do was kiss and carry her back to bed. However, he knew they had too much to settle first.

"I love you so much and was determined to make you mine. I didn't take the time that I should have to earn your trust. You should have never had any doubt about my response to anything you had to tell me. I didn't give you that opportunity and I'm so very sorry. Will you please forgive me?"

Brooke's eyes filled with tears and Brice bowed his head. He brought their hands to his mouth and kissed her palms. He was fighting hard to keep his own emotions from overtaking him. He wanted to show Brooke strength, but in reality, he was scared. Scared she wouldn't forgive him. Scared she still couldn't trust him. Scared he would lose the ground he'd gained.

She pulled her hands free, and Brice raised his head. Brooke threw her arms around him, burying her face in his neck. She nodded and spoke incoherently into his neck as she cried. Brice picked her up and carried Brooke into the living room where he sat on the sofa with her on his lap.

After several minutes passed, Brooke raised her head, looked into his eyes and said, "There's nothing to forgive." She kissed him as though her life depended on it. After coming up for air, Brooke leaned her head against his. "Do you have anything you want to ask me?"

"Several things, but let's start with how long have you been sick and the specific diagnosis and prognosis."

"What?" Brooke's face twisted. "How did you find out about that?"

"After I put you to bed Friday night, I accidently kicked over your bag and all these pill bottles came rolling out. I know I shouldn't have but I got curious so I did some research."

"Research?"

"Yes, the drugs for fatigue, depression, pain and numbness can treat a lot of things. As I started reading, the one consistent theme I found was treatment for an autoimmune disease."

Brooke slid off his lap and stood in front of the window. Brice could see she was struggling with something, but he wasn't going to push. He needed her to know he wasn't going anywhere, no matter what she said.

Brooke released an audible sigh and turned to face him. "I have multiple sclerosis, or MS."

Brice offered a supportive smile, nodded slowly but remained quiet. He had thought that might be it, but hearing her say it out loud made him thankful he was still sitting down. While Brice was relieved to finally know what was going on, he was anxious to hear how she was doing.

"I was diagnosed several months ago. My foster brother, Peter, is my doctor and my prognosis is good. There hasn't been too much damage to my nervous system. For the most part, I've been symptom-free, but when I do have a flare-up, I have a very specific treatment plan that gets me over the hump."

Brice stood. "I can't begin to explain just how proud I am to call you my wife." He walked up to Brooke and pulled her into his arms. "I'm so sorry you had to go through all this by yourself. Never again." In that moment Brice vowed to himself that he was going to do everything in his power to ensure she stayed healthy and happy.

Brice's cell phone rang. "You should get that. We'd hate a repeat of this morning."

"Good point." He gave her a quick kiss, released her and walked into the kitchen to find his phone.

"He still doesn't know about my past," she mumbled to herself, as pain began to shoot up her spine. "I have to tell him right now."

"That was Alexander. He was just checking to make

sure we were all right after Mother's visit." He placed his phone on the coffee table.

Brooke nodded. "Brice, I need you to sit down."

"What's wrong?"

"Please." She gestured toward the sofa.

Brice frowned. "Okay," he replied, sitting on the sofa's edge.

Brooke returned to the chair across from Brice. She knew he'd physically try to comfort her as she tried to explain things he needed to know, which would only distract her. "You asked about Perez and the blackmail."

"Yes. I don't see why he thinks my not knowing about you having MS would cause any major problems for us or our company. It doesn't make sense."

"You're right, it doesn't. He's not blackmailing me because of my MS." Brooke stared down at her hands.

"Then what else is there?"

Brooke pushed out a quick breath, raised her head and met his fixed gaze. Brice's visible anxiousness that had disappeared after hearing about her MS diagnosis had returned and so had Brooke's fears about his response to her past.

"Before I changed it, my name was Brooke Avery and for eighteen months, between graduating high school and my freshman year of college, I was a high-end escort."

Brice's face was expressionless and unresponsive to her words. Brooke wasn't sure if he'd stopped breathing or simply gone into shock. "I swear that I never once had sex with any one of my clients."

Brice sat back and dropped his shoulders. "What else?"

Brooke took a deep breath and released it slowly, adjusting in her seat, trying to ease the pain in her lower back. She filled Brice in on her life during that time and the role Shannon had played. Brooke gave a detailed account of her arrest, why she'd changed her name and the initial blackmail attempt, including the doctored evidence against her.

Brice leaned forward, resting his forearms on his knees. "You were blackmailed once before and instead of telling me everything then, you chose just to leave me. You let someone end our marriage without a fight."

"I thought I was protecting you and your family. Plus..."

"Plus what?"

"I'd just been diagnosed and told that children might not be possible. With my luck that might mean no. I know how much you want to have a child so..."

"So, what..."

Brooke wiped her tears that were rolling down her face. "I figured you could find someone else that could for sure give them to you."

Brice rose from his seat, came and knelt before Brooke. He cupped her face and brushed away her tears with the pads of his thumbs. "I'm so sorry if I ever made you think you were supposed to be some kind of baby-making machine. Yes, I want to have children, but I want to have them *with* you. Not necessarily from you."

Brooke's brows creased and her face flushed. She was feeling confused and the pain had spread to her torso, which made her ability to concentrate that much more difficult. "I don't understand."

"Sweetheart, when the time comes for us to have children, we will weigh all of our options. I am a very wealthy man. With wealth comes responsibility *and* choices. If we can't have biological children, we'll adopt. You are my great love and life partner. I'm sorry if I failed to make you realize that."

As difficult as it was, Brooke wrapped her arms around Brice's neck, buried her face in his chest and cried. Brice rubbed her back. After a few minutes, her tears subsided and Brice picked her up and carried her back to the sofa.

"Ouch…" Brooke cried out, gripping his arms.

"What's wrong?" Fear transformed his face.

"MS…my chest…hurts."

"I should get you to the hospital."

"No hospital." Brooke could hear the panic in his voice.

"What do you want me to do? Should I call Peter?" Brooke could see the distress in Brice's eyes and it was breaking her heart. "No…get…my pills."

Brice ran into the kitchen, grabbed Brooke's pill bottles and a glass of water. He returned and sat on the side of the sofa where Brooke was now lying, holding her arms around her body.

"What do you need?"

Brooke pointed at three of the bottles he held. "Two… from each…one," she whispered.

He handed her the pills and Brooke couldn't help but notice the slight shake of his right hand. Brice helped her sit up and fed her the requested dosage. "Are you sure you should be taking all these pills?"

Brooke offered him a weak smile. "I'm sure. I'm going…to be asleep…soon."

"I'll take you upstairs." Brice picked up Brooke and cradled her in his arms.

"Stay with…me…awhile?"

"Only for the rest of my life," he whispered.

Chapter 22

Brice carried her to the bedroom and sat her on the bed. "Do you need help getting undressed?"

"I… I'm afraid…so," she admitted.

"Lay back, my love."

Holding his gaze, Brooke did as he requested. Brice unzipped Brooke's jeans and caught sight of her red lace panties. He had to fight to stay focused on the task at hand because his wayward body instantly responded. Brice removed her jeans and tossed them to the side. He leaned over her. "Let's get that top off too." He unbuttoned her blouse and a red lace bra with the front snap showcased her beautiful breasts and her erect nipples peeking through the lace. "Damn," he whispered. Brooke gifted him with a small smile.

"Are you…okay?" she asked, staring up at Brice, her eyes scanning his face.

Brice tried to present a poker face, failing miserably.

"I'm fine." He raised her upper body slightly and removed the blouse.

"You don't…look fine," she said.

"Don't worry about me. How do you feel? You sound a little better." He pulled the covers over her.

Brooke sighed. "Weak, but getting there."

"On a scale of one to ten, how do you rate the pain?"

"It's about a nine, down from fifteen," she said.

"Are you sure you don't want me to call Peter?"

"I'm sure. What I'd like for you to do is hold me,"

Brice joined her on the bed, staying above the covers and wrapping his arms around her. "Baby, can I ask you something?"

"Anything." Brooke snuggled into him.

"How often do you have these attacks?"

"Stress is a trigger, so more often since I got back."

Brice tightened his arms around her. "I'm sorry." Brooke leaned back and proclaimed as forcefully as she could, "My flare-ups aren't your fault."

Brice kissed her hair and pulled her back into his chest. "I appreciate you saying that, but I disagree."

"Perez is the primary cause, but we'll bring him down tomorrow."

"Yeah, about that…"

"What about it?" she asked, her voice barely above a whisper.

Brice could tell Brooke was getting sleepy and he didn't want to upset her anymore but he wasn't going to let anyone, including his family, hurt her ever again.

"We'll talk about it later. Go to sleep."

"Okay," she whispered.

After nearly an hour, Brice slid his half-asleep arm out from under Brooke. He slowly got out of the bed to ensure he didn't wake her. Brice made sure she was sound asleep before he went into the closet to retrieve the envelope with all the false evidence she'd told him about and made his way back downstairs. Brice opened the envelope and examined all the material and even though he knew none of it, except for the arrest report, was real, Brice's heart broke. Not because of what the fake evidence portrayed but for the pain it had caused Brooke.

Brice found his phone, stood in the middle of his living room and placed a call he knew he'd have to explain later to a very angry Brooke.

"Hello," a strong baritone voice answered.

"What's up, A? Can I talk to you for a minute?"

"Sure, I can talk. What's up?"

"It's about tomorrow." Brice started pacing the room.

"What about it?"

"I don't want Brooke meeting with Evan Perez alone."

Alexander exhaled noisily. "Brice, I understand how you feel but don't you think that's a decision Brooke should be making?"

"A, she's sick, man. She can't handle the stress and she'll never admit that, either."

"I'm guessing you talked to her."

"Yeah, she has MS." His voice dropped an octave.

"I'm sorry, man."

"Yeah me too, but her prognosis is good."

"Well, that's something," Alexander stated.

"That's everything and I want it to stay that way. Coming face-to-face with Perez could make things worse."

"What do you mean?"

"I mean, stress is one of her triggers," Brice said.

"Triggers?"

Brice could hear the confusion in his brother's voice. "Yes. Stress can trigger an MS flare-up and before you ask what that is, it can mean different things to different people but for Brooke, she has trouble breathing and can be in a lot of pain and have a host of other symptoms."

Brice stopped pacing and looked up at the ceiling. "She's upstairs medicated and sleeping right now because of an episode after telling me all of this."

"So, she told you everything?"

Brice took a seat on the sofa. "Yes, finally. The thing is, she thought I knew about her past when I was talking about her being sick."

"Oh, man."

"So after we discussed the MS she told me about her history with Shannon and how it connected her to Perez, the blackmail and she even told me about the doctored pictures. It took everything I had in me to stay still and hear her out. Because all I wanted to do—"

"Was find him and cause him as much pain as he'd caused her, right?"

"Right."

"That's how I felt after China's car accident. Remember what you told me?"

Brice dropped his head in his left hand while he held the phone to his right ear. He knew what words were about to be fed back to him. "Yes," he responded, hoping that would be good enough. It wasn't.

"You told me to let the security team handle things regarding China's accident when I wanted five minutes alone with the driver."

"That was different," Brice insisted.

"How so?"

"China was safe with you. What you wanted was revenge."

"And you don't?"

"Hell yeah, I do. For everything he's put us all through, but not at the risk of my wife."

The phone fell silent. "I get that. What do you have in mind?"

"I know if I tried to convince Brooke to stay away, she won't do it, so I need to be there with her," Brice stated.

"If Perez sees you, he'll know something's up."

"I know. He won't see me and neither will she."

"What are you saying?"

"I'll stay out of sight in the kitchen at the restaurant. The only people who will know I'm there are Meeks and his team."

"Do you really think you can watch Brooke with Perez and not react?" Brice heard his brother's doubtful tone.

"I have to."

Brice could feel Alexander's apprehension and worry coming through the phone. He knew it would be hard to watch Brooke put herself in danger, but he also knew she was going to do it with or without him. The only way he could remotely deal with it was if he was there.

"All right."

"I'll keep it together," Brice promised.

"I hope so. This may be our last shot at getting that bastard. What do you need from me?"

"Talk to Meeks and Mother for me."

"Oh, no. I'll handle Meeks. Mother's all yours." Alexander laughed. "I'll call you back in a few."

Brice walked in the kitchen and pulled a beer out of the refrigerator. He twisted off the top and took a long pull. Brice needed a little added courage for the next conversation he was about to have. After finishing off his beer, he sat at the island and called his mother.

"Good afternoon, son. How's Brooke?"

"She's not doing too well. Did you know she was sick too?"

"Yes, she told me after explaining her connection to Perez," she answered nonchalantly.

"Dammit, Mother, why didn't you tell me? Why did you choose now to stay out of my personal life?"

The phone fell dead and Brice dropped his head. He took two deep breaths and called his mother back. "Victoria Kingsley," she answered.

"Mother—"

"So, you do know who you're talking to."

"Yes, ma'am, and I apologize."

"Better. Now, to answer your ill-constructed question, you weren't there when Brooke had to explain to me, her mother-in-law, that she'd once been a high-end escort—"

"She didn't have sex with those men."

"Of course, she didn't, son. But she was still an escort and she did get arrested. Imagine the humiliation she felt and maybe even fear. I'm told I can be scary sometimes."

"Sometimes…"

Victoria remained silent. Brice heard music in the background so he knew she hadn't hung up again. "Sorry, Mother."

"Brooke showed courage coming to me with this mess, so when she asked me not to tell you, to give her the chance to do it herself, I happily obliged."

"Yet, you told Alexander."

"Of course, I did. Perez is not only attacking our family, he's coming after our business…my business. I will not let him get away with that. It's time to bring his tyranny to an end and, thanks to Brooke, that happens tomorrow. You should be very proud of her. Thank you, James," he heard his mother say to her longtime assistant.

"I am very proud of her, but I'm also scared for her safety," he admitted.

"Don't be ridiculous. The meeting is being held inside the airport restaurant where you have to pass through metal detectors just to get to it, and the place will be full of people. The location couldn't be safer. Brooke has already shown in multiple ways how strong she is in spite of having MS. Hell, you boys could learn a thing or two from that woman. I hope you get off your butt and make sure she stays your wife."

Brice had every intention of ensuring that, but first, he had to keep her safe. "I plan to, Mother, and the safety of my wife comes first. With that being said, I can't let Brooke confront Perez alone, and hear me out before you say anything."

"I'm listening."

Brice laid out his proposal to Victoria, stressing the fact that he would stay out of sight and wouldn't jeopardize the plan. He felt like a kid again, explaining to his mother the reason he needed to go on a camping trip she'd already said no to. Only this time, he wasn't taking no for an answer, no matter what she said.

"All you boys get that protective instinct from your father. Did I ever tell you about the time when your father and I were taking a road trip and I needed to go to the ladies' room so we stopped at a roadside gas station?"

"No, ma'am, I don't think so."

"Let's just say your father paid everyone to leave so I would have privacy and he could be sure I was safe."

Brice laughed. "Sounds like Dad. He always said men protect their queens."

"That he did," she agreed.

"That's all I'm trying to do; protect my queen."

Victoria sighed. "Fine. But you make sure you follow Meeks Montgomery's instructions to the letter and stay out of sight. I want Brooke to be safe, but I also want that bastard out of our lives once and for all."

"I agree, and I will. Thanks, Mother."

"I love you, son."

"Love you too," he replied before disconnecting the call.

Now that his revised plan was in place, Brice decided he wanted to spend the rest of the night taking care of his queen. But there was something he had to do first. He picked up the folder with the false evidence against Brooke and moved over to the sink. He pulled out a lighter from the drawer and lit the photos on fire. He stood and watched as the lies Perez had visually created dissolved into ash while he was trying to tamp down the anger building inside. He washed the ash down the drain before he grabbed his phone and made his way downstairs to work off the anger he couldn't repress.

After nearly an hour of pounding out his frustrations on his punching bag, he went upstairs and checked on his sleeping wife before taking a quick shower. He noticed that he'd missed a call from his brother. Brice changed into a pair of long black shorts and a white T-shirt and called his brother.

"Sorry I missed your call, A," he said, going to stand next to the bed and looking down at Brooke.

"No problem. I just wanted to let you know I talked to Meeks. While he wasn't happy about you being present on scene, he certainly understood. He has firsthand knowledge about having a wife put herself in danger."

"Yes, he does. I'm not sure I'm man enough to handle that on a daily basis," Brice admitted.

Alexander laughed. "Me, either. I guess some of Dad's attitude rubbed off on us after all."

"Yeah, Morgan didn't get it all."

Both men laughed. "Mom called," Alexander informed him.

"Yeah."

"Looks like we're all set for tomorrow. Just keep it cool."

Brice looked down at the sleeping beauty in his bed. He thought about all she'd been through because of Perez and slowly nodded his head, knowing his brother couldn't see him. "I have no choice. Brooke deserves justice, and I won't do anything to interfere with that unless Perez does something to try and hurt her physically."

"I understand, but the way things are set up in that restaurant, Meeks's people will pounce on him if he even twists wrong."

"I'm counting on it."

The brothers said their goodbyes and Brice spent the rest of the night nursing and hovering over Brooke. When she finally woke, he brought her dinner in bed. There was no discussion about the past or what the future might bring, only the promise they'd always be by each other's side. When Brooke fell back to sleep, he watched over her until his body surrendered to its own need for a rest.

Chapter 23

The smell of freshly brewed coffee woke Brooke from the most peaceful night of rest she'd had in months. Brooke opened her eyes, took a deep breath and exhaled it slowly. She stretched out her arms and found Brice's side of the bed empty. She wasn't a bit concerned after the glass-house-like treatment he'd given her last night, from waiting on her hand and foot when she was awake to wrapping his arms around her in bed and literally rocking her to sleep.

Brice had always insisted that it was not only his job but his pleasure to take care of her when she wasn't feeling well. Brooke was happy to see that hadn't changed. While the opportunities for him to do so in the past had been few, she feared their future could be very different. *Stop it. Remember what Brice said. We're going to take whatever MS has to offer one day at a time; only from now on, we're doing it together.*

Brooke sat up, swung her feet over the side of the bed and commenced doing her morning circulation exercises.

She was rotating her hands and feet when Brice entered the room. "Good morning, beautiful," he greeted her, walking in holding a cup of coffee. "How do you feel?"

"Good morning to you too, handsome, and I'm fine," she countered, admiring the expensive blue suit he wore. She looked at the side table clock. "It's after seven. I should get a move on." She accepted the cup.

"Not so fast. There's been a slight change in plans."

Brooke took a drink from her cup, having a feeling she was going to need the caffeine. "What changed? What did you do, Brice?" she asked, giving her husband the side-eye.

"Me? Nothing. Meeks, on the other hand, has had to make a few adjustments to today's plan."

"What adjustments?"

He leaned down and kissed her on the forehead. "It's no big deal. Just enjoy your coffee and get dressed and meet us downstairs."

The doorbell rang. "That's them now."

"What's going on, Brice?"

"Let me get them settled, and I'll be back to explain everything. Trust me. Please," he stated as he left their bedroom.

Yes, Brooke, it's time to trust Brice. She got up and drank her coffee as she continued her morning ritual. In spite of everything that was happening, Brooke felt like her old self again, and she knew it had everything to do with being back with Brice and having everything out in the open.

Brooke stood in the middle of her closet, ready to get her day started. "Today definitely calls for the blue Chanel power suit." She dressed, stepped her feet into Chanel shoes and pulled down the matching purse. She gave herself the once-over in the mirror and said, "Well, at least the outfit still says Brooke Kingsley don't play."

"No, she doesn't," a low baritone voice added, walking into the closet. "And she's very beautiful."

Brooke turned to face Brice and smiled. "You're biased."

"I am, but it's also true." Brice leaned in and kissed her on the lips. "You ready?"

"As I'll ever be."

"Good. I'd like to talk to you about something before we head downstairs."

"All right." Brooke wasn't sure what was going on, but she wasn't worried. Whatever it was, they would deal with it together. Brice offered her his left palm and Brooke placed her right hand in it, which he then brought to his mouth. He kissed it before leading her out of the closet and back to the bedroom.

"You okay, baby?" Brooke saw concern in Brice's eyes and she smoothed away his worry lines.

"Yes, I'm fine."

"What's up?" Brooke sat down on the bed.

"Meeks and his team are setting up for the call downstairs."

"Downstairs, why?"

"He's just being cautious, because Perez fired his man on the inside this morning."

"Why?"

"They don't know, and until they figure that out, they thought it would be best to run this part from here."

"From here…in a house?"

"Just the first phase. You'll still have the meeting at the airport."

Brooke released an audible sigh. She couldn't stand the idea of Perez being in her house. "That's fine." She looked at the clock. "It's after eight. We should get started."

Before Brooke could move, Brice said, "There's one more thing."

"What now?"

"I don't want there to be any more secrets between us—"

"There aren't. I swear I've told you everything." Brooke's heart skipped several beats at the idea of Brice not believing her.

"I know you have, baby." Brice ran the fingertips of his left hand across her lips. "I'm the one who must tell you something."

"What?"

Brice explained the role he'd be playing in today's sting, and Brooke felt such a sense of calm come over her that all she could do was throw her arms around Brice's neck and kiss him. When they finally came up for air, Brooke said, "Thank you."

"Wow. Not quite the response I was expecting, but I'll take it," Brice admitted.

"What were you expecting?"

"Oh, I don't know, that maybe you thought I was being overprotective or something for insisting that I be there on-site during the meeting."

Brooke placed her right hand over her heart. "Heavens no, honey, you're just trying to protect me. I get that. To be honest, knowing that you'll be in the next room makes me feel even better. It makes me love you even more."

Brice smiled. "I love you too. Let's go."

Brooke grabbed her things and went downstairs. Brice and Brooke walked in to find that their dining table had been converted into a makeshift office with several different types of computer systems set up.

"Good morning, everyone," Brooke greeted.

"Mrs. Kingsley," Meeks and his team chorused.

Brice followed Brooke into the kitchen with Meeks and Robert behind him. Brice walked over to the refrigerator and pulled out a pitcher of orange juice. He retrieved two glasses from the cabinet. "Can I get you anything?" he asked Robert and Meeks as he poured juice into two glasses.

"No, thank you. I'd like to go over a few details about the call," Robert said.

Brice handed Brooke her glass. "Sure thing. Brooke, take your medicine."

"Yes, sir." Brooke gave Brice a two-finger salute. "What details?" Brooke questioned, taking her pills.

"When you speak to Perez, you tell him you need reassurance that he won't try to come after you again."

"I can do that," Brooke stated, finishing off her juice.

"You have to convince him you have a lot to lose by doing what he wants."

"What's going on?" Brice asked, frowning.

"We're not sure if he's just being paranoid or thinks something's up because not only did he fire our inside person, he also fired his whole team. The only people from his inner circle he's keeping around are Shannon, his own security team and a couple of lawyers he's had for years."

"With everything Perez has done I bet he is paranoid." Brooke dropped two slices of bread in the toaster. "You sure I can't get anyone anything?"

"No, we're fine," Robert replied. "The system is up and running. You can make the transfer now or whenever you want."

The toast popped up. Brooke took a couple of bites, brushed the crumbs from her hand and said, "Let's get this over with. What system do you want me to use?"

"I don't." Robert handed her a small tablet.

"You want me to transfer millions of dollars to an overseas account using a tablet. Is that even possible?"

"That's not just a tablet. It carries my very own programs," Robert claimed proudly.

"We gave them temporary access to our system as well," Brice informed his wife.

"I don't understand why I couldn't just log in using my own access right here," Brooke inquired.

"Because my algorithm is proprietary," Robert said.

"Oh, okay… Where's the list?"

"You don't need it. I've programmed all the numbers into that system. All you have to do is log in and hit *send* basically." Brooke followed his instructions and their homepage of their office bank popped up. As promised, the list of accounts and the associated amounts were already populated and ready to go. "Here goes nothing." Brooke hit the *send* button and watched their account drain. "Done."

"Now what?" Brice asked.

"Now, we wait for Shannon's call," Meeks advised.

Brooke went to the refrigerator and pulled out the butter and jelly. She dressed the rest of her toast, put everything away and sat at the island to eat.

"Meeks, is everything ready at the restaurant?" Brice questioned, checking his watch.

"Yes, and we'll head over as soon as the time is set."

They didn't have to wait long. Brooke's phone rang, but before she could answer it, Robert handed her another one identical to her own. "What's this?"

"We cloned your number so we can record the call. Answer it and put it on speaker," Robert ordered.

"Hello."

"What the hell do you think you're doing?" Shannon yelled.

"Well, good morning to you too."

"Cut the crap. Where's the rest of the damn money?"

"There's been a change of plans." Brooke could feel everyone's eyes on her.

"Look, Brooke—"

"No, Shannon, you look. I'm not sending out another dime until I talk to your partner. I believe his name is Evan Perez."

The phone fell silent. Brice came and stood behind Brooke, wrapping his arms around her waist. Brice thought he was offering her his strength and support when in reality he was keeping himself from losing it and saying something that would blow the plan.

"Hold on," Shannon said. Brooke heard her muffle the receiver.

"Brooke Avery," a deep voice said.

Brice felt Brooke shiver and he tightened his hold. "It's Brooke Kingsley now."

"That it is. You wanted to speak with me."

"Yes, but not on the phone. I'm sure you don't want our business discussed on an open phone line."

"You haven't forgotten everything Shannon taught you. Good girl. You and me alone somewhere, now that's an intriguing thought."

Brooke squeezed Brice's arms and he knew she was signaling that she was fine. "I meant someplace public. After what happened Friday night, I'm not willing to be alone with you or anyone else from your crew."

"Yes, well, I understand things got a little out of hand."

"A little…"

"I'm not sure what we have to discuss. Shannon tells me you understand what's expected."

"Either we meet so I'm sure that you know what *I* expect or you take what you've got already and be satisfied with that."

"My, you're tougher than Shannon said you were and looking at your photos, very beautiful." Brice's breathing escalated.

"Are we meeting or what?"

The phone fell silent again and the room went still. "Where are we meeting? I hear you have an affinity for the zoo. Let's say eleven."

Brooke glanced at Meeks and Robert to confirm the time was okay, and they both gave her the thumbs-up. "Eleven is fine, but not at the zoo."

"Where?"

"The Seafood Kitchen in Hobby Airport."

The phone fell silent again and Brice held his breath. He couldn't imagine sending Brooke out to meet this man alone. Thank goodness, he didn't have to.

"See you there, but let's make it eleven thirty." The call dropped.

Brooke sucked in a quick breath and turned in Brice's arms, hugging him as if she needed to reassure herself that he was still there. "Are you all right?" he whispered.

"No, I'm not, but I will be."

"Excuse me, Brooke," Robert interrupted.

"Yes," she replied, turning to face him.

Robert picked up the phone. "I need you to keep this with you."

"Why?"

"It has state-of-the-art tracking and the recorder is voice-activated," he explained.

"She'll be at the restaurant, so why is that necessary? I thought that place was bugged everywhere." Brice's confusion transformed his face.

"It is, but we can't control the noise level in the restaurant to the point that it doesn't appear natural," Meeks said.

"Natural?" Brooked asked.

"Yes. People speak at differing volumes, so if we make everyone's conversations in the room too low, Perez will get suspicious. Placing the phone on the table isn't unusual for people these days and it will amp up the sound," Robert explained.

Meeks checked his watch. "We'll head to the airport in about an hour. You should come with us," he said to Brice.

"What about Brooke?" Brice questioned.

"I'll be fine."

"Yes, she will, because she'll ride over with my team. Don't worry, we still have eyes on the street," Meeks informed Brice.

"I'd feel better if she came with us," Brice stressed.

"That's not a good idea. She needs to be seen entering the airport alone. Trust me. He'll have someone watching."

Brooke faced Brice. "I'll be perfectly safe. It's almost over."

Chapter 24

After seeing Brice and Meeks's team off, and in an effort to work off some nervous energy, Brooke busied herself cleaning the already immaculate house, which took all of fifteen minutes. She tried to watch the TV but couldn't focus on anything, so she ditched that idea. Brooke settled for pacing the room and watching the clock while she waited for her escorts to arrive. When both her cell and the cloned phone rang, Brooke jumped. *Chill.* Brooke picked up the phone and read the screen.

"Hi, Lori."

"How are you?"

"I'm fine," she snapped.

"Okay…"

"Sorry, I'm just a little nervous and ready to get this over with," Brooke explained, adjusting a picture that was already perfectly straight on a wall.

"I'm sure. Do you need anything?"

"No, I'm good. Thanks for checking," she replied as

her phone beeped. Brooke checked the screen and smiled. "Sorry, Lori, that's Brice. I have to go."

"I take it things are good." Lori couldn't hide the excitement in her voice.

"Better than good, but I'll have to fill you in later." Brooke switched over to Brice's call. "Hi."

"Hi. How are you?"

"Better now. Meeks has his team passing by the house every fifteen minutes."

"Good." Brooke could hear the relief in Brice's voice and that made her smile.

"How are things there?"

"I must say, they have this place decked out perfectly. You'll be completely safe."

"I figured as much, but it's nice to hear it, anyway," she admitted.

"Your escort should be there—"

The doorbell rang. "They're here—"

"What?"

"Hold on." Brooke walked to the door with the phone at her side. "What are you doing here?"

"You said you wanted to talk in person. Well, here I am. There's no time like the present."

Fear paralyzed Brooke for several moments as she stood face-to-face with her worst nightmare, until she remembered who she was, all she'd been through and survived. Brooke had no doubt that backup would soon arrive. *You can do this.*

"You're right. Please," Brooke stepped aside and gestured with her hand for him to enter. "Come in."

"Nice place you have here," he complimented her.

"Thank you, Mr. Perez."

"Please, call me Evan. Most of my business partners do."

"Oh, so that's what we are, business partners," she replied. No matter how distinguished he looked in the expensive suit he'd decked his large fit frame in or how neatly cut his salt-and-pepper hair was, Brooke feared how dangerous he could be if he didn't get what he wanted.

"What else would you call it?"

"Excuse me." Brooke held up her phone so he could see it. She was trying to be as natural as possible. "You caught me in the middle of something."

"Please, continue. I'll just have a seat. Make myself comfortable."

Brooke stepped a few feet away from him, so he couldn't hear both sides of the conversation she was having. "Sorry about that, Lori. I have an unexpected guest. I'll have to call you back."

"We're on the way, sweetheart," Brice replied. She could hear the panic in his voice.

"No worries." Brooke ended the call and placed the phone on the coffee table.

"Can I get you something to drink?"

"No, but I'd like you to sit with me."

Brooke sat in the chair across from him. "I heard you were one of Shannon's girls that wasn't receptive to the new direction we wanted to take the business. It would have afforded you a life of real luxury."

"No, I wasn't. I never wanted any part of that new world."

"Yet, somehow you managed to achieve it all on your own." His eyes scanned the various expensive artworks that decorated their walls. "I guess me and my friends were a little too old for you."

"Can we get down to business?"

"Yes, of course. Only half of your job is complete." Perez shrugged as if there was nothing else to talk about.

"I need to be sure you won't try to come for me ever again."

"I guess you're going to just have to trust me," he said, sucking his teeth.

"That's not good enough."

Perez narrowed his eyes and tilted his head slightly. "Excuse me."

Brooke channeled her mother-in-law's spirit and said, "You're so good at creating affidavits, I want one of my own. I want something in writing that says definitively that all the previous statements were false and the photographs were doctored. I don't care how you do it. Just make it happen or you won't see another dime."

Perez puffed out his chest and glared at Brooke. "You obviously don't know who you're talking to, little girl."

"I know exactly who I'm talking to, Mr. Evan Perez. I will not let you keep blackmailing me with a bunch of lies so you can destroy an innocent woman and her family."

Perez jumped up, grabbed Brooke by her arms and pulled her into his chest. "Innocent family," he yelled. Perez held up the pinky finger of his right hand. That's when she noticed the tip was gone. "That so-called innocent woman did this…herself. She destroyed my business…my reputation. It took years to come back from it, and Victoria Kingsley is going to pay. If that means destroying you in the process, so be it."

Perez threw Brooke back down in the chair. "Look—"

"Shut the hell up. Now I came here out of goodwill to try to work this out. Do things the easy way."

"Goodwill?" Brooke adjusted herself in the chair.

"Yes, but that doesn't seem to work with you, so here's what's going to happen." His eyes roamed over her body. Brooke began to shake with fear, because she knew that look; she'd seen it before, in the faces of men whose sexual requests she'd denied, and she only prayed that Brice would get there in time.

"First, you're going to transfer the rest of my damn

money." He took off his jacket and went and sat down on the sofa. "Second, you're going to come over here and ride me until I'm good and satisfied, because your ass is mine."

Brooke stopped breathing and tears rolled down her face. Perez smiled. "Oh, yeah, keep crying. That's just how I like it. In fact—" he checked his watch "—I got time and you can make the deposit after. Get over here."

Brooke sat still as a statue. He'd have to kill her first. "Never!" she tried to scream, but the word came out barely above a whisper.

He said, "I'm waiting…"

Brooke wrapped her arms around herself, clamped her legs, mouth and eyes shut. It was the only thing her pain-riddled body and fear-plagued mind would allow her to do as a form of protection.

"Hell no," she heard a female voice yell at the same time as loud commotion and shuffling sounds filled the air. Before Brooke could react to what was happening, she was up and out of the chair and into arms that she knew instantly.

"Brice," Brooke whispered, opening her eyes.

"I got you, sweetheart." Brooke looked around the room, which was now filled with police, Meeks's security team and men with FBI jackets on. Perez was in handcuffs and being led out the door as someone was reading him his rights.

"What…happened?" Brooke questioned as Brice sat her down on the sofa.

"Are you in pain?"

"Yes, I need…my medicine."

"I'll get them." Brice tried to move away from Brooke; only she wouldn't let him go. She knew she was being ridiculous. The danger was gone and she was safe in her own home, but she couldn't stand the idea of being away from Brice for even the few moments it would take to get the medicine she needed so desperately. "Don't leave me."

* * *

"Mr. Kingsley, where are they? I'll get them for you," one of Meeks's female agents offered.

Brice felt relieved, because he wasn't prepared to leave Brooke's side, either. He told the agent the location and which pills she needed. Brice took a seat next to Brooke and placed his arms around her waist.

"I'm sorry. I just…"

"I understand, my love." Brice kissed her temple.

"What the hell happened?" Victoria demanded as she entered the room, wearing an army green pantsuit, looking like the commander-in-chief she was. "Where was her protection?"

"How the hell did he know where we lived?" Brice asked no one in particular.

The agent returned with Brooke's pills and handed her a glass of water. "Thank you," Brooke replied.

"No problem, ma'am."

Brooke took her pills and drank half the glass of water down before handing it to Brice. "I want to know how he got past the security gates."

"Please, everyone, calm down, and I'll share what I can," Meeks announced. Victoria took a seat on the other side of Brooke.

"It appears that Perez changed his plans but didn't bother to tell his team since they showed up at the airport as planned. We had them picked up too, by the way."

"Good," Brice said.

"I don't understand. What, he didn't trust his own team?" Victoria asked.

"That wasn't it. What Robert managed to get out of Perez—" everyone glanced over at Robert, who smirked and was massaging his right hand with his left "—was that he wanted something extra from Brooke that he couldn't get from her in public."

Brice could feel his anger rising to the surface all over again; only he reined himself in when Brooke leaned further into him. He knew he had to keep it together for her.

"That bastard—he tried the same thing with Elizabeth years ago," Victoria advised.

"But you made him pay," Brooke said.

"Yes, I did. Elizabeth didn't want to involve the police, which was fine with me. You don't put your hands on things or people that don't belong to you, especially a Kingsley." Victoria's venom was on full display and the room's temperature seemed to drop a few degrees. She took a deep breath and released it slowly. Victoria turned her body to face Brooke. "Are you all right, my dear?"

Brooke reached for her hand. "I am now. It's over and our family is safe."

Victoria kissed Brooke on the cheek, then stood. "Is it over?" She turned her attention to Meeks. "Do you have everything you need to bury that bastard in a deep dark hole?"

"Yes. Brooke did a great job keeping him talking until he snapped. There's no doubt he'll be going away for a very long time."

"And your money has already been returned, Mrs. Kingsley," Robert informed.

"Good. You never know when a storm may roll in."

"We're going to clear out, but you'll need to make an official statement in a day or two," Meeks advised.

"No problem, and thank you for everything," Brooke said.

Brice rose from his seat and offered his hand. "Yes, thank you."

After Brice saw everyone off, he carried Brooke upstairs, which was when Brooke noticed that he was wearing his wedding ring; an antique eternity band with five-carat black-and-white bezel-set diamonds. Brooke's heart started racing, even though she knew she shouldn't read anything into it. While Brice finally knew her whole truth, and she'd apologized for keeping him in the dark, she had run and broken his heart.

Brice placed Brooke on the bed, and he sat down next to her. "I can't tell you how proud I am of you. But are you okay?"

"Yes, I'm fine. Can I ask you a question?"

"Always."

"Why are you wearing your wedding ring?" She picked up his left hand and ran her thumb over it.

Brice's face lit up and a slow sexy smile spread across his lips. "Because the last time I checked, I was still a married man. And frankly, I missed it."

Brooke didn't even try to hide the tears that fell from her eyes. She lowered her head and whispered, "Me too."

Brice captured her chin between his thumb and index finger and raised her head. Brooke met his gaze. "Would you like yours back?"

"Yes—yes," she stuttered.

Brice reached into his pocket and pulled out the ten-carat mate to his ring. He held it between his fingers of his right hand. He offered his left palm to Brooke. She felt besieged by her feelings and her heart was beating so fast she couldn't believe Brice didn't hear the blood rushing through her veins. Brooke wiped away her tears and presented her left hand.

"You can have this back on one condition," he offered.

"Which is?"

"That you never take it off again." Brice's eyes captured hers.

Brooke could see uncertainty cross his face but she was so overwhelmed with emotion she couldn't get any words of reassurance out. She gripped his hand, brought it to her heart and shook her head like a bobblehead doll.

Brice smiled. "I'll take that as a yes." He took the ring and slipped it back onto her finger. Brice brought the ring to his mouth and kissed it.

"I… I love you," Brooke finally managed to get past her lips.

"That's good, because I love you too, my forever bride."

* * * * *

KIMANI™
ROMANCE

COMING NEXT MONTH
Available February 20, 2018

#561 TO TEMPT A STALLION
The Stallions • **by Deborah Fletcher Mello**
Marketing guru Rebecca "Bec" Marks has had eyes for Nathaniel Stallion from day one. Regardless of Nathaniel's naïveté to her crush, her ardor for the newly crowned restaurateur remains intact. And when her romantic plans are threatened, she'll pull out all the stops to prove she's his soul mate…

#562 HIS SAN DIEGO SWEETHEART
Millionaire Moguls • **by Yahrah St. John**
Hotel manager Miranda Jensen needs to marry to inherit her grandfather's fortune. The treasurer of the San Diego Millionaire Moguls chapter, Vaughn Ellicott, offers her the perfect solution. Until she begins to fall for their pretend affair. Will Vaughn choose to turn their make-believe marriage into a passionate reality?

#563 EXCLUSIVELY YOURS
Miami Dreams • **by Nadine Gonzalez**
When Leila Amis meets her new boss, top Miami Realtor Nicolas Adrian, their explosive attraction culminates in a brief fling. Then their affair ends in bitter regrets, leaving Nick heartbroken. A year later, he's back with an irresistible offer. With even more at stake, can Nick make Leila his forever?

#564 SOMETHING ABOUT YOU
Coleman House • **by Bridget Anderson**
Pursuing her PhD while working at her cousin's bed-and-breakfast and organic farm leaves little personal time for Kyla Coleman. Until she meets Miles Parker. There's something about the baseball legend turned food industry entrepreneur that captivates her. When a business opportunity comes between them, can Miles persuade Kyla he's worthy of her trust?

Want to give in to temptation with
steamy tales of irresistible desire?

Check out **Harlequin® Presents®,
Harlequin® Desire** and
Harlequin® Kimani™ Romance books!

New books available every month!

CONNECT WITH US AT:

Harlequin.com/Community

 Facebook.com/HarlequinBooks

Twitter.com/HarlequinBooks

Instagram.com/HarlequinBooks

Pinterest.com/HarlequinBooks

ReaderService.com

**ROMANCE WHEN
YOU NEED IT**

PGENRE2017